AF226424

Zero Honor

A Pentagon~CIA Conspiracy Thriller

The Shadows of State Book 2

By
DR. NAEEM MEO

Copyright 2026

All right Reserved

ISBN: 978-1-971178-05-9

DEDICATION

Inspired by my wife and dedicated to heroes whose history never names.

ACKNOWLEDGEMENT

The Shadows of State – Zero Honor was written with an understanding that some stories live in the shadows—not because they lack importance, but because truth is often inconvenient. This novel reflects the difficult questions that arise when justice, fear, and power collide.

I am grateful to the readers who are willing to sit with moral uncertainty and consider the human consequences behind political decisions. To those who believe that heroism does not always come with recognition, this story is for you.

My deepest thanks go to my family and friends for their patience and support while I explored a narrative shaped by loss, endurance, and compromise.

Above all, I acknowledge the power of storytelling—to imagine the lives history may never fully record, and to give voice to those who endure their sacrifices in silence.

DISCLAIMER

The Shadows of State – Zero Honor is a work of fiction. While it draws inspiration from real historical events, global conflicts, and post-9/11 geopolitical realities, all characters, dialogues, operations, legal proceedings, and intelligence activities portrayed in this novel are fictionalized. Any resemblance to real persons—living or deceased—or to actual events beyond broadly known historical facts is coincidental.

The depiction of intelligence agencies, military personnel, detention facilities, legal systems, and counterterrorism operations is intended solely for narrative purposes. This novel does not claim to represent factual accounts, classified information, or verified actions of any government, organization, or individual.

The story does not seek to accuse, defend, or expose any real-world institution or person. Instead, it explores fictional scenarios to examine the moral ambiguity, political pressure, and human cost that can arise during times of global fear and conflict.

This work should be read as a fictional exploration of sacrifice, secrecy, and survival—not as a statement of historical or political truth.

TABLE OF CONTENTS

CHAPTER 1:
THE REAL CHALLENGE

Winning permission from the district court judge to transfer Aadil Gul from Guantánamo Bay to the Northern Neck Regional Jail in Warsaw, Virginia, was a monumental victory for Ashley, the young public defense attorney who had refused to give up. The courtroom erupted with congratulations. Her colleagues, her mother, and even Aadil's family celebrated the first real step toward bringing him home. For the first time in years, hope felt tangible.

But Ashley knew better than anyone that this was only the beginning.

Getting Aadil onto U.S. soil was one thing. Fighting for his freedom was another. Ahead of her loomed the impossible task of defending a man accused in a 9/11 terrorism case while standing against the full weight of the United States government. The path would be dangerous, exhausting, and unforgiving.

Yet Ashley felt no fear.

She would do anything, absolutely anything, to free her husband.

During the transfer period, Ashley meticulously prepared the case. She interviewed family friends who had shared weekly dinners with Aadil. Every testimony painted the same picture: a man of integrity, loyalty, and honor. All of them were willing to vouch for him.

The first step was done. Aadil was close. The next challenge loomed: securing bail and preparing for trial. Ashley was already organized, determined, and fearless.

It was her first official case, and it was personal.

Martha had explained the legal terrain to her clearly. Terrorism cases were handled in federal district courts under federal law, often tied to the USA PATRIOT Act and Title 18 of the criminal code.

Because of its role in handling many 9/11-related cases, the Eastern District of Virginia would oversee Aadil's trial. As a U.S. citizen, he could not be tried by a military commission. His case belonged in civilian court, with a federal district judge presiding and the U.S. Attorney's Office leading the prosecution, often with support from the Department of Justice's National Security Division.

Ashley understood exactly what she was walking into.

The day of the first hearing arrived quickly.

The marble walls of the Eastern District Court of Virginia seemed to hum with tension. Cameras flashed outside, but inside the courtroom, silence reigned, broken only by the faint shuffle of papers and the echo of footsteps across the polished floor. Ashley adjusted her blazer, her heart pounding, as Aadil was brought in by two U.S. Marshals. His wrists were cuffed, his face pale but composed.

Judge Henderson, known for his unflinching approach to terrorism-related trials, took his seat at the bench and acknowledged the case of United States versus Aadil Gul.

Ashley rose. Her voice was calm, but her resolve was unmistakable. She entered a plea of not guilty on her client's behalf and requested his release on bond pending trial. She emphasized that Aadil was a U.S. citizen with a permanent address in Washington, D.C., a record of good behavior during detention, and no history of violence. He posed no threat to the community. She reminded the court that he had already endured more than two years in harsh conditions at Guantánamo Bay without any substantiated evidence linking him to the 9/11 attacks.

The government prosecutor, Mr. Jenkins, stood immediately. His tone was clipped and firm as he opposed bail. He argued that Aadil was a high-profile detainee connected to Bin Laden, classified as a former war combatant, and a potential national security risk. Releasing him, even under supervision, could endanger public safety.

A murmur rippled through the courtroom.

Ashley tightened her grip on her pen but did not waver. She countered that the prosecution's claims were built on assumptions rather than facts. Aadil had no record of violence, no disciplinary issues during detention, and no means of flight. As a U.S. citizen, he was entitled to due process under the Constitution.

She then raised another issue. The discovery package, she explained, was incomplete. The government had released only surface-level interrogation records from Guantánamo and Bagram. There were no transcripts and no raw intelligence logs. She formally requested full discovery.

Judge Henderson turned his gaze toward Mr. Jenkins, who assured the court that the complete discovery would be provided.

After a long silence, the judge spoke. Given the gravity of the allegations and the potential risks, national security had to take precedence. Bail was denied. Aadil would remain in federal custody pending further proceedings. The next hearing was scheduled for sixty days later.

The words landed heavily.

Ashley had expected the outcome, yet it still cut deep.

As Aadil was escorted out, she requested a brief meeting. The judge allowed a few minutes in a conference room before the marshals returned him to custody.

Inside, the space felt smaller, the fluorescent lights harsh. Aadil sat across the metal table, cuffs still on. Ashley forced a small smile and told him this was not what they had hoped for, but it was only the beginning. The first hearing was always difficult. The judge had acknowledged his citizenship, and that mattered.

Aadil nodded quietly. He told her he had seen worse and did not want her getting into trouble for fighting his case.

She softened. That was her job, she said. She had promised his mother and herself that she would bring him home.

A faint smile tugged at his lips. He told her she had not changed, still stubborn.

She laughed through tears and admitted she was not planning to.

A knock came at the door. Time was up.

Ashley gathered her papers and told him she would see him soon. Next time, she said, they would be ready.

As the door closed behind him, she stood alone for a moment, staring at the empty chair. The echo of the judge's decision still rang in her ears, but louder still was the promise she had made to herself.

No matter how deep the shadows, she would bring him back into the light.

CHAPTER 2:
BUILDING THE DEFENSE

The night sky over Washington, D.C., blurred with soft rain against the courthouse glass. Inside her small, dimly lit office, Ashley sat surrounded by piles of folders, files stamped "CLASSIFIED," "CONFIDENTIAL," and "RESTRICTED ACCESS." The air smelled faintly of coffee and printer ink.

It had been three days since the bail hearing. The denial still weighed on her, but she refused to stop. Martha, her senior colleague, walked in carrying two cups of coffee and a large binder.

"You've barely slept, have you?" Martha asked.

"Not really," Ashley replied. "I keep replaying the hearing in my head. I know the judge made the right call based on what's in front of him, but he hasn't seen the truth yet."

Martha set the coffee down and flipped open the binder. "That's exactly what we're going to show him."

Ashley sighed. "I don't like Mr. Jenkins."

Frustration tightened her voice as she continued. "He looks mean. Cold. Almost evil. Martha, why are all these DA prosecutors like that? They act as if justice belongs only to them. Arrogant, untouchable, no conscience at all."

Martha didn't answer right away. She took a slow sip of her coffee, watching the shadows stretch across the room.

"Because, Ashley," she said at last, "they've got something we don't. Power. And worse, they've had it for too long. When you're sitting behind the Department of Justice seal, backed by the full weight of the U.S. government, you start to believe you are the law, not just enforcing it."

Ashley frowned and shook her head. "That's not justice. That's intimidation. They have unlimited resources, investigators, analysts, and surveillance, and we have a small office and a paralegal. It's not fair."

Martha gave a dry smile. "Fairness doesn't exist in the DOJ's vocabulary. You'll see. The abuse of power is quiet, polished, and procedural. They'll call it national security, but really it's about control."

Ashley lowered her voice, thoughtful but edged with anger. "And the judges? Aren't they supposed to be the balance, the conscience of the system?"

Martha leaned forward, resting her elbows on the table. "In theory, yes. But in practice, most federal judges favor the government. Always have. Remember, they come from the same ladder, former prosecutors, state attorneys, deputy AGs. They speak the same language."

Ashley looked stunned. "You're saying even judges are political?"

"Completely," Martha said. "Every decision they make, every ruling, every speech, is about political point scoring. Today they're on the bench, tomorrow they're running for Senate or campaigning for a governorship. Justice isn't blind in America, Ashley. It's negotiated."

Ashley's eyes narrowed. "I can't believe that's how the system really works."

Martha gave a weary smile, her tone both cynical and wise. "Believe it. Every judge, every prosecutor, every so-called neutral official, they're all on the U.S. government payroll. And they know which side they're expected to favor. Their job isn't always to find the truth. It's to make sure the government doesn't lose."

Ashley fell silent, her gaze drifting toward the window, toward the D.C. skyline glittering under the evening lights. She whispered, almost to herself, "Then we'll just have to make them see the truth anyway."

Martha looked at her for a long moment, recognizing that stubborn spark, the same fire that once burned in her when she was young. "That's exactly why you might just win this, Ashley. They intentionally gave us an incomplete discovery package. They only released surface-level interrogation records from Guantánamo and Bagram. No transcripts. No raw intelligence logs."

"Which means they're hiding something," Ashley said.

"Exactly," Martha replied. "Or they're waiting for us to make a mistake before they drop it in court. We've already filed a motion for full disclosure, and hopefully we'll get it soon. DA prosecutors always play that dirty trick."

Ashley leaned back, rubbing her temples. "Martha, if they classify everything under national security, how do we defend him?"

"By using what isn't classified," Martha said. "The timeline. His U.S. citizenship. The letter he sent from Saudi Arabia. The inconsistencies in the CIA's version of his capture. They're painting him as Bin Laden's second man, but there's zero evidence of command authority. That's where we hit back."

Ashley nodded slowly. Her mind was already mapping out the angles. Prove Aadil wasn't in New York or Afghanistan during 9/11. Show his forced recruitment under ISI supervision. Highlight the torture at Bagram and the lack of due process.

"We'll build the story of a man caught between two wars," Ashley said quietly. "One political. One personal."

Martha smiled faintly.

Ashley glanced at a photograph on her desk, her father in uniform, smiling beside her on her law school graduation day. His Pentagon connections had helped open doors, but she wanted to win this on merit, not favors.

A light knock came at the door. The paralegal, Lisa, stepped inside. "Ashley, I compiled all the case references you asked for. Hamdi v.

Rumsfeld, Rasul v. Bush, and the Boumediene decisions. They all deal with detainees' rights. You can argue jurisdiction and due process."

Ashley flipped through the folder, impressed. "Good work, Lisa. These precedents are our backbone. The Constitution doesn't stop at Guantánamo's fence line."

Later that night, after everyone else had left, Ashley stayed behind. The rain outside had turned into a steady downpour. She opened Aadil's file again, the interrogation report, the medical record from Bagram, and the faded photo of him before 9/11. The smile in that picture was almost unrecognizable compared to the broken man she had seen behind bars.

She took a deep breath and began typing her motion for full due process protection.

"Every individual, regardless of location or accusation, is entitled to fundamental fairness under U.S. law. The government cannot claim secrecy as a shield for silence."

Her hands trembled slightly as she signed her name.

Ashley Smith, Defense Counsel for Mr. Aadil Gul.

CHAPTER 3:
THE GENERAL'S WARNING

The night was heavy with silence. Washington, D.C., shimmered under a blanket of cold October rain as Ashley drove toward her uncle's residence near Arlington. The moment she stepped into General Robert's study, she could smell the faint trace of cigar smoke and leather, the scent of authority and old wars.

He sat behind his mahogany desk, still in his crisp uniform shirt, shoulders broad and posture perfectly straight despite his age. Maps of the Middle East were pinned to the wall behind him, Afghanistan, Pakistan, Saudi Arabia, places Ashley now associated with pain rather than geography.

"Uncle Robert… I need your advice," Ashley said.

Her voice trembled slightly, but her eyes were steady. "You've worked with the Pentagon. You know how they think. What do you suggest?"

The General studied her for a long moment, not as a soldier or an officer, but as a man who had watched too many people break under the machinery of power. He leaned back in his chair.

"Ashley, being as close to your family as I am, I'll tell you the truth," he said. "I don't want you to lose this case. And I don't want you to destroy yourself trying to win it the wrong way."

Ashley frowned. "You think I can't win?"

"I think you're standing against a mountain," General Robert replied. "The government, the CIA, the Pentagon, they don't lose terrorist cases. Even when they're wrong."

He paused, his voice low and deliberate. "They have too much power. Too much to protect. They can twist facts, shape narratives, erase truths. And when they can't win in the courtroom, they win in the shadows."

"What if the prosecutor brings up Aadil's connection to 9/11?" Ashley asked. "What if they try to make him a scapegoat?"

"I'm already aware of your growing concerns," he said calmly.

He leaned back again, his expression composed but tired. He had seen too much of the system from the inside to pretend it was pure.

"Ashley," he said quietly, "Washington already knows Aadil had nothing to do with 9/11. The CIA knows it. The Pentagon knows it. But after a tragedy like that, the public needs someone to blame. Billions of dollars flow into intelligence and defense. People need to believe their money is fighting something real."

Ashley stared at him, stunned.

"It's the same pattern everywhere," he continued. "Look at Guantánamo. Most of those men were just in the wrong place at the wrong time. But politics isn't about justice. It's about perception. Your job is to show the truth, that Aadil wasn't one of them. Keep it simple. Keep it clean."

His words chilled her, not because they were harsh, but because they felt true.

That conversation became a turning point for Ashley. She realized she wasn't just defending a man. She was standing against an entire narrative built on fear and convenience.

"I've read the discovery," General Robert said. "I've gone through the Pentagon memos, the CIA reports, all of it. You and I both know what's in there, and what's not."

Ashley nodded slowly. "There's nothing conclusive. No confession. Just suspicions and assumptions."

"Exactly," Robert said, folding his hands. "But if you start accusing the government, the CIA, the Pentagon, Homeland Security, if you even hint that they made a mistake or covered something up, they'll crush this case before you can finish your first sentence. They'll turn the courtroom into a battlefield."

Ashley looked down, her voice barely a whisper. "So what do I do, Uncle Robert?"

He leaned forward, his tone low and deliberate. "You tell a story, Ashley. A believable one. Something simple. Something the court can accept without shaking the foundation of Washington. Forget about exposing the system. That's not how you win. You win by giving them a way to save face while still letting your client walk free."

He paused, letting his words settle. "This whole 9/11 aftermath isn't just about justice. It's about saving face. The CIA and the Pentagon have already been humiliated for not capturing Bin Laden. They need scapegoats. And once they have one, they don't let go."

"You need to create a simple story," he continued. "Don't touch the CIA. Don't mention the Pentagon. Don't make this political."

Ashley looked up, conflicted. "But it's not the whole truth."

Robert's voice softened, though his eyes remained firm. "Truth doesn't always win, Ashley. But strategy does. The truth comes later, when you've survived."

For a long moment, the only sound was the ticking of the old brass clock on the wall.

Finally, Ashley closed her folder and nodded. "You're right. I'll rewrite everything. Aadil was in the wrong place at the wrong time. Nothing more."

Robert allowed himself a small smile. "Good girl. Remember, you're not fighting facts anymore. You're fighting power. And power doesn't forgive those who embarrass it."

He poured a glass of water and handed it across the desk. "Let the discovery help your story. It already supports it, the gaps, the vagueness, the missing witnesses. Use all of it to your advantage."

Ashley took the glass, her hand trembling slightly. "You really think this will work?"

Robert leaned back again, his expression unreadable. "It must. Because if it doesn't, the people you're fighting won't stop with just Aadil."

Her voice dropped to a whisper. "So what do I do?"

The General turned, his eyes sharp and calculating, the look of a man who still knew how to fight wars that weren't on paper.

"Make a deal."

Ashley blinked. "A deal? With the Pentagon?"

"Yes," General Robert said. "Let me handle it. Quietly. I still have people inside. You keep fighting in court. Show the world you're standing for justice. But don't push too hard against the system. Don't attack the CIA or the Pentagon directly. Keep your case simple. Aadil was trapped in the wrong place at the wrong time. That's your story."

"You think that will help?" Ashley asked.

"It might save his life," he replied. "The prosecutors might go for the death penalty or life in prison. They'll make him look like the second man to Bin Laden to justify their failures. I'll do what I can through my channels. Get someone to listen. Maybe open a quiet door for negotiation. But remember, say less. Don't talk too much about national security or government misconduct. Just survive the storm."

Ashley stared at him, absorbing the weight of his words, then slowly stood.

"Then I'll make sure it works," she said quietly. "Thank you, Uncle Robert. I'll follow your advice."

As she left his office, the General watched her go, the faint light of his desk lamp glinting off his medals. He gave a faint smile, the kind soldiers give when they know a battle hasn't been won, only postponed.

"You're a brave girl, Ashley," he murmured to himself. "But bravery alone doesn't win wars. Strategy does. Let me handle the strategy."

As Ashley stepped back into the rain, the weight of his words settled over her like armor, and like a warning.

CHAPTER 4: PENTAGON, SECURE OFFICE WING

General Robert stepped through the thick steel doors of the Pentagon, greeted by the low hum of voices and the rhythmic click of boots echoing on polished floors. He was not in uniform today, just a dark suit and a badge that still granted him quiet access to the places where real power lived.

He entered a conference room where two men were already waiting: Colonel Raymond Hill, a Defense Intelligence liaison, and Deputy Director Mitchell, one of the CIA's legal advisers. They exchanged polite nods, but the air was heavy with unspoken truths.

"I'm not here to challenge your operations," General Robert said. "I'm here to talk reason."

Mitchell raised an eyebrow. "This is about your niece, the lawyer from the Eastern District?"

"Yes," Robert replied. "And her client, Aadil Gul. The so-called second man to Bin Laden."

Hill scoffed. "That man's lucky he's still breathing. Do you know how many chains of command had to approve his transfer from Gitmo? We did him a favor."

"Then maybe you'll do one more," Robert said. He leaned forward, his voice low. "He's innocent. You've got the wrong man. The evidence is hollow. The only thing he's guilty of is being too close to the wrong people."

Mitchell folded his hands. "The government's narrative can't change now. We've already filed statements with the DOJ and issued media briefings. The public believes he was part of Bin Laden's inner circle."

"Then quietly correct the record," Robert said. "Move him to a secure domestic facility, reduce the charges, something."

He lowered his voice further. "If this case goes public and it turns out the U.S. tortured an innocent citizen for years, it won't just embarrass your agencies. It will bury them."

Silence followed. Hill shifted uneasily. Mitchell exhaled, his eyes narrowing.

"We'll see what we can do," Mitchell said at last. "Off the record."

"That's all I ask," Robert replied.

As he left the Pentagon, Robert knew he had stirred the hornet's nest, but it was the only way.

Back at the courthouse, Ashley sat in a conference room with Martha, reviewing the discovery documents again and again, searching for gaps.

"See this section?" Martha said, pointing to the thin paragraph describing Aadil's capture. "No witnesses. No visual proof. No forensic trail. Just hearsay from two anonymous informants, probably Taliban."

"Exactly," Ashley said. "And yet they call him second to Bin Laden. There's nothing here but assumptions and fear."

"Fear wins cases," Martha said quietly. "Especially when the government is holding the torch."

Ashley closed her folder. "Not this time. Not if I can help it."

Her phone buzzed. A secure message from her uncle appeared on the screen.

Keep your head down. They're listening. Work quietly. Trust no one.

She looked up at Martha and forced a calm smile. "Let's get to work."

Later that night at Northern Neck Jail, Aadil lay on his cot, staring at the faint light flickering through the barred window. The sound of distant rain reminded him of Islamabad, of nights spent sitting on the roof with his mother, drinking tea and watching lightning dance over the hills.

He thought of Ashley, her voice, her courage, the way she had cried in Guantánamo. For the first time in years, he allowed himself to hope.

A guard's voice echoed down the corridor. "Mail call. A letter for Gul."

Aadil sat up. The envelope was small, white, neat, and faintly jasmine scented.

Stay strong. We're fighting for you.

Ashley.

He closed his eyes and whispered, "For the first time, I believe it."

The small attorney conference room was quiet except for the faint hum of the overhead fan. Ashley leaned forward across the table, her legal pad open, pen ready. Aadil sat opposite her in a beige prison jumpsuit, his wrists free but still marked with faint scars from years of restraint.

"Alright, Aadil," Ashley said gently. "Now we need a justifiable explanation for why you were in Afghanistan. The judge will ask that right away. When exactly did you leave the United States for Pakistan?"

"Three days before 9/11," he said. "That's what I told you before."

"Good. And your passport? Do you still have it?"

"No," he said, shaking his head. "I lost it somewhere in Afghanistan."

Ashley paused, her eyes narrowing thoughtfully. "That's actually good. There's no direct trail or travel history connecting you. Let me think about how to justify your presence there."

Aadil leaned forward. "I have an idea. Maybe we can say one of my friends was kidnapped two months before 9/11. The kidnappers took him across the border into Afghanistan and demanded ransom."

"Go on," Ashley said.

"They were Taliban," Aadil continued. "I went myself to pay the ransom and bring my friend home. After I paid them, they killed him anyway. Then they captured me, too. To protect themselves, they told the U.S. Army that I was part of Bin Laden's security team."

Ashley's eyes lit up slightly. "I like that. It's logical and believable. Kidnappings were common in Pakistan before and after 9/11. The Taliban often hid victims across the border. The CIA already knows that pattern. It fits."

"Exactly," Aadil said. "Even after 9/11, groups like that kept kidnapping people for money or messages. They hid in caves and villages, especially near Tora Bora. That region became a haven for anyone running from the Americans."

Ashley nodded, writing quickly. "Good. Very good."

She looked up again. "Tell me something. Are you familiar with Afghanistan and the northern parts of Pakistan?"

"Yes," he said. "Very familiar. I worked in those areas before. I know the border regions, Kunar, Nangarhar, Tora Bora, even parts of Waziristan."

"Then tell me honestly," Ashley said. "Where do you think Bin Laden might be hiding now?"

Aadil hesitated. "If I had to guess, Pakistan. After Tora Bora, it was too dangerous to stay in Afghanistan. He couldn't go back to Saudi Arabia. The safest place would be inside Pakistan, probably protected by ISI. That's just my guess."

"That makes sense," Ashley said. "And we'll leave that out of the official record. I think we're in a good position unless the U.S. Army has secret evidence or a signed confession from you."

"What's the worst-case scenario?" Aadil asked.

"Right now, everything is fifty-fifty," she replied. "We won't mention your ISI background or any link to Bin Laden. That would complicate everything. We keep it simple. Wrong place, wrong time."

"And if they ask about my work before this?"

Ashley smiled faintly. "You helped me at home, cooked, and ran errands. You were quiet, respectful, and law-abiding. I don't think they'll dig that deep. And if they do, I'll handle it."

They both stood as the guard waited near the door.

"Thank you, Ashley," Aadil said softly. "I love you. Take care."

"I love you too," she replied. "Stay strong. I'll see you soon to discuss the discovery further."

CHAPTER 5:
PREPARING FOR TRIAL

The meeting room at the Northern Neck Regional Jail was cold and sterile, its fluorescent lights casting a pale glow on the white concrete walls. The heavy steel door closed behind Ashley, sealing her into silence.

Then Aadil walked in, and for the first time in months, he looked different. Healthier. His beard was trimmed, his eyes clearer, and there was even a faint smile tugging at his lips. He looked, Ashley thought, almost like the man she had married.

"You look good, Aadil," Ashley said gently. "Are you getting some sleep now?"

He nodded. "Yes. For the first time in years. The food is better here, too. And I don't wake up to shouting every night."

Ashley smiled faintly as she opened her leather briefcase and took out a stack of papers.

"I received the discovery this morning," she said. "It's surprisingly short."

She handed him the top page. "It says you were arrested twenty miles north of Tora Bora, based solely on information from local villagers. They told the U.S. Army you looked suspicious, that you might be part of Bin Laden's security detail."

"That's it?" Aadil asked, frowning.

"That's it," Ashley said. "There's nothing in the report about you confessing or admitting anything. The entire case is built on what the locals said. Then it lists the charges: terrorism, conspiracy, aiding Bin Laden, and the 9/11 attacks. Thirty counts in total."

Aadil exhaled slowly, running a hand through his hair. "How serious are those charges, Ashley?"

"They're as serious as it gets," she replied calmly. "But remember, charges are not proof. The burden of evidence is on the government. They must prove every count beyond a reasonable doubt. Our job is to create doubt. And there's already a lot of it."

"How will the prosecutor defend these charges?" he asked.

Ashley leaned forward, tapping her pen lightly against the paper. "They'll try to use testimony from the Army, maybe the general who led the operation near Tora Bora. They might even call a few intelligence officers. Their goal will be to connect you to Bin Laden's inner circle. But they'll have no physical proof of it. No photos. No recordings. No direct evidence. Only assumptions and field reports."

"Will they bring the general to testify?" Aadil asked.

"They can, but I doubt it," Ashley said. "The Pentagon hates exposing internal operations in open court. They'd rather settle quietly than risk cross-examination. My job will be to question every witness they bring, to expose the contradictions, the missing evidence, the weak chain of custody."

Aadil nodded slowly, absorbing her confidence. "And how will the judge decide?"

"In cases like this, especially under national security," Ashley said, "the judge can go two ways. Either assign a regular jury or appoint a special tribunal of three to five expert judges. It depends on how the government frames your case, as a civilian matter or as a war crime tribunal. We'll know at the initial hearing."

"Do you think it'll go to trial?"

"If the government realizes their evidence is thin, they'll settle," she said. "And that's exactly what I'm aiming for. A full trial would expose their weak case, and they don't want that kind of press."

Ashley took a deep breath, then smiled softly. "I've already prepared my opening statement. I've also reached out to several of Dad's friends who used to join our family dinners. They'll write character reference letters. They remember you well. Those letters will help establish who you truly are, not what the Army says you are."

She stood, smoothing her suit jacket, then reached back into her briefcase and pulled out a small garment bag, handing it to him.

"I brought a suit for you," she said. "Wear it on Monday. The judge should see the man I know, not a number in a file."

Aadil held the bag carefully, as if it were something sacred. "Thank you, Ashley. For everything."

"Get some rest," she said, her smile tinged with sadness. "I'll see you in court on Monday, nine sharp. Everything will be fine. Trust me."

"I trust you," he said quietly. "Take care."

As the guards escorted him back to his cell, Ashley lingered a moment longer in the room, staring down at the discovery papers. Just a few pages, yet they could decide a man's life.

She gathered her files and whispered to herself, "They don't know what's coming. Not this time."

CHAPTER 6:
THE FIRST HEARING

The courtroom of the Eastern District of Virginia was packed that morning. Reporters sat quietly in the back rows, pens ready. The air was thick with anticipation, a rare case involving a man once accused of being tied to Bin Laden himself.

At precisely 9:00 a.m., the heavy wooden door opened, and the bailiff announced, "All rise. The Honorable Judge William H. Carver presiding."

Judge Carver, tall and composed, with years of federal experience behind his sharp eyes, took his seat. Everyone else followed.

Ashley straightened her blazer, her heartbeat drumming in her ears. Her mother sat in the second row beside General Robert.

The clerk called the case. "United States versus Aadil Gul, case number 03-427."

Aadil, wearing a dark blue suit and a red tie, stood beside Ashley at the defense table. His posture was straight, his expression calm, but his eyes searched for reassurance. Ashley gave him a slight nod.

Judge Carver looked down from the bench. "Counsel, we will begin with the government's opening statement."

Assistant U.S. Attorney John Jenkins rose deliberately, buttoning his black suit jacket. His voice carried authority and precision.

"Your Honor," he began, "this case concerns one of the darkest chapters in American history, the terrorist attacks of September 11th, 2001, which took the lives of nearly three thousand innocent men, women, and children.

"The defendant, Mr. Aadil Gul, was captured in the mountainous region near Tora Bora, Afghanistan, the very area where Osama bin Laden escaped U.S. forces.

"At the time of his arrest, the defendant was reported to be wearing the same type of uniform as members of bin Laden's personal security detail.

"The government firmly believes he was a trusted member of that circle, a man who aided and abetted the mastermind of 9/11.

"We therefore ask this Court to treat him as what he is, a danger to the United States and its people, and to impose life imprisonment without parole."

A hush fell across the courtroom.

Ashley stood slowly and confidently, adjusted the microphone, and began to speak. Her voice was calm yet firm, carrying the weight of both love and conviction.

"Thank you, Your Honor.

"The prosecutor just described a tragedy that broke every American heart, including mine. I was in Washington, D.C., that morning. I remember the fear, the smoke, and the silence afterward. I know what that day means to this country.

"But this case, Your Honor, is not about 9/11. It is about one man, a husband, a son, and a U.S. citizen, who was simply in the wrong place at the wrong time.

"Mr. Gul's presence in Afghanistan was not for conspiracy or terror. It was an act of desperation and humanity. He traveled there searching for his kidnapped friend, who had been taken across the border by local militants demanding ransom.

"As this Court is aware, Pakistan and Afghanistan have been hotbeds of kidnapping for ransom cases for decades. I have submitted official reports from both the State Department and Interpol confirming that fact.

"When my client attempted to pay the ransom and rescue his friend, he was ambushed by the same group, robbed, beaten, and nearly killed. Within hours, local villagers, fearing American drones and seeking favor with U.S. troops, falsely claimed he was part of bin Laden's guard.

"That is how this man was captured, Your Honor, based on fear, confusion, and hearsay."

She paused and placed several documents on the judge's bench.

"These are sworn character statements from six distinguished individuals: retired U.S. generals, a former ambassador, and a former defense minister, all of whom personally knew Mr. Gul from 1999 until shortly before September 11th. They describe him as kind, respectful, intensely loyal to the United States, and utterly opposed to extremism.

"They dined with him. They spoke with him. Not one of them ever saw a trace of radical behavior."

Judge Carver briefly scanned the top page, an eyebrow lifting slightly.

Ashley continued. "Your Honor, the government's discovery provides no evidence, no photographs, no communications, no eyewitnesses, nothing linking my client to any act of terror. Even their own records fail to mention any confession or statement by Mr. Gul.

"I urge this Court to see through the fog of fear and politics. This man is innocent. He was trapped by circumstance, a civilian lost in a war zone.

"We respectfully request that the Court dismiss all charges of terrorism or, at a minimum, grant a fair trial based on facts, not assumptions."

Her voice softened as she concluded. "This nation is built on justice, not vengeance. My client has already endured three years in a war prison, tortured and isolated for crimes he did not commit. It is time to let truth, not emotion, guide this courtroom."

Judge Carver looked toward the prosecution. "Does the government have witnesses or evidence to contradict the defense claims?"

The prosecutor rose again. "Your Honor, based on the discovery, the government has strong evidence and witnesses, which will be presented during the jury trial."

Judge Carver leaned back, fingers steepled beneath his chin. "Thank you, Ms. Smith. The Court will take these statements under advisement. The next hearing for witness review and evidence examination will be scheduled in thirty days.

"Given the nature of this case and its significance to national security, I have decided to proceed with a special jury trial. Due to its classification as a war crimes and terrorism matter, a standard civilian jury will not apply."

The courtroom stirred quietly as he continued. "Instead, this Court will appoint three senior judges, each with extensive experience in federal criminal, military, and international law, to serve as a special jury panel. They will evaluate all evidence, hear testimony, and deliver a collective verdict in accordance with U.S. and international legal standards.

"The trial will commence in sixty days. Both parties are expected to submit final witness lists and all remaining discovery within four weeks."

Ashley stepped forward again, her notes steady in her hands. "Your Honor, my client was caught in a severe misunderstanding. Mr. Gul tried to escape from kidnappers hiding in a village loyal to Bin Laden and the Taliban. Fearing for their own lives, the villagers handed him over to the U.S. Army, claiming he was a Bin Laden bodyguard. But a Pakistani-born U.S. citizen as Bin Laden's personal security? Does that make sense?"

Judge Carver nodded, listening closely.

"His only fault was being in the wrong place at the wrong time while trying to save his friend," Ashley continued. "From June 1999 to May 2001, Mr. Gul was a law-abiding U.S. citizen. He has six character certificates: three from retired U.S. Army generals, one from a retired ambassador, one from a retired defense minister, and one from his mother. All are present in this courtroom today."

She paused, making eye contact with the bench. "My father, a former ambassador, passed away in 2002. My mother is here to support Mr. Gul. This is a clear case of mistaken identity. Mr. Gul has always been loyal to the United States. He despises extremism and is willing to cooperate fully with the government. I respectfully request dismissal or, at a minimum, release on bail."

The judge leaned back, considering her words. Then he spoke. "Very well. Mr. Gul will be released on bail today. The government has sixty days to present substantial evidence at trial. I expect efficiency and seriousness from both sides."

Ashley nodded. "Thank you, Your Honor."

As the gavel struck, ending the session, Aadil turned to her, his eyes glistening. "You were incredible," he whispered.

Ashley smiled faintly, unable to speak. Across the room, her mother and General Robert exchanged relieved looks.

Outside the courthouse, camera flashes erupted as they stepped into the daylight. Reporters shouted questions, but Ashley kept walking, her briefcase clutched tightly to her chest.

Inside it, she carried hope and the beginning of a strategy that could change everything.

Ashley's hands trembled as she hugged Aadil, who was grinning broadly for the first time in years. Tears streamed down his face, mirrored by Ashley's mother and the family friends nearby.

The prosecutor's expression hardened. He said he respected her position but urged her to reconsider, adding that it might be the only way to save her client's life.

Ashley left the office with her chest tight and her thoughts racing. The weight of the case pressed down on her, but she refused to compromise the truth.

She stepped outside and immediately dialed her uncle's number.

When General Robert answered, Ashley told him everything. She explained that the prosecution was threatening to use a retired general as a witness to force Aadil into a guilty plea and that they were offering life imprisonment in exchange. She admitted she had refused but did not know what they would do next.

Her uncle told her not to worry. He said they had anticipated a move like this and assured her he would handle it. There were ways, he said, to neutralize the impact of such a witness. He instructed her to focus on preparing her case and to leave anything involving the Pentagon or the CIA to him. They would not let the government corner her or Aadil.

Ashley thanked him, her voice steadying as some of the tension eased. She told him the jury trial was going to be intense.

He agreed, but reminded her that she was smart, prepared, and had the truth on her side. They would get through it.

After the call ended, Ashley returned to her work. She spent the rest of the day reviewing every detail of the case, reinforcing her arguments, and preparing herself for a courtroom battle that could decide Aadil's fate.

The stakes had never been higher, but she refused to let fear dictate her actions. Justice and the truth about Aadil would prevail.

CHAPTER 8:
THE LAST TRUMP CARD

Thursday morning, the Pentagon was unusually quiet, the kind of silence that only precedes something monumental. Inside a classified operations chamber, deep beneath the building's fortified floors, General Robert sat at a long metallic table. The air was cold and heavy, filled with the faint hum of hidden surveillance equipment.

Moments later, two of the most powerful men in America entered: the Director of the CIA and the Chairman of the Joint Chiefs of Staff. The doors sealed behind them with a coded lock. No aides, no recorders, no written notes. Only three men who understood the stakes.

General Robert stood and saluted briefly.

"Gentlemen," he began, his voice low but commanding, "I need a full update on our progress in locating Usama bin Laden. It's been years since Tora Bora. What do we really know?"

The CIA Director adjusted his glasses, glancing at the encrypted screen on the wall. "We've followed several trails, most of them cold. Sporadic signals from the tribal belt near the Pakistan border, but nothing verifiable. We believe he's constantly on the move with ISI protection. Every drone sweep has come up empty."

The Chairman of the Joint Chiefs of Staff added, "We've lost men and resources chasing ghosts. The intelligence network in that region is fractured. Even our allies feed us misinformation."

General Robert exhaled slowly, his hands clasped behind his back. "That's exactly why I asked for this meeting. You're chasing shadows, gentlemen, and in the process, the government is crucifying an innocent man to cover the embarrassment of our failure."

The room fell silent. Both men knew he was referring to Aadil Gul.

General Robert continued. "The man you're holding, the one accused of being bin Laden's bodyguard, was never his operative. He was collateral, caught between Taliban politics and our own desperation. If this case continues, we'll turn an intelligence mistake into a national scandal."

The CIA Director frowned. "And your solution?"

Robert leaned closer, his voice measured and firm. "We need to change the narrative, now. I can provide you with a strategic solution that accomplishes two objectives: protecting classified operations and ensuring that wrongful prosecution ends quietly. But it requires total discretion and cooperation from this room only."

The Chairman of the Joint Chiefs exchanged a cautious look with the CIA Director. "Go on."

Robert outlined his plan, a calibrated mix of intelligence redirection, classified reclassification of field reports, and selective leaks that would steer attention away from Aadil's name. It would give the appearance that the CIA was still pursuing the real operatives while discreetly clearing Aadil of direct involvement.

When he finished, there was a long pause. Finally, the CIA Director nodded slowly. "Your method...it's unconventional, but it's clean. You've just given us a way out of a political trap."

The Chairman of the Joint Chiefs leaned back. "You've always had a knack for solving problems that others can't even talk about."

Robert's eyes hardened. "Then let's act before Monday's hearing. The clock is ticking. Once the truth is out, it cannot be undone."

The CIA Director extended his hand. "Thank you, General. You've done your country and us a great service."

General Robert shook both of their hands firmly. "Just remember, this stays between us."

As he left the Pentagon, the corridor lights reflected off his polished boots. He carried the weight of what he'd just done, bending the truth to save justice.

For Ashley. For Aadil.

And for a country that didn't always know when to stop fighting its own shadows.

He paused, then continued with the quiet authority of a man who had seen this before.

"Ashley, this is typical. When the government wants to bury someone, they don't run out of shovels. They can create new evidence, new witnesses, new reports, all signed, stamped, and sealed. And the court... well, the court will listen to them."

Ashley leaned back, closing her eyes. "So what do we do now?" she whispered.

There was a long silence before Robert replied.

"You pray. Pray that those witnesses never make it to the stand. Because if they do, no one, not even me, can save him."

Ashley's throat tightened. "Uncle Robert..." she murmured, barely holding back tears.

His voice softened. "Don't lose faith, child. Sometimes the truth needs more than courage. It needs timing. Leave the rest to me."

Ashley nodded, wiping her eyes, even though he couldn't see her. "Thank you, Uncle Robert. I'm not telling Aadil or Mom. They've both been through enough."

"Good," Robert said quietly. "Let them sleep in hope tonight. You and I will carry the worry."

The call ended. Ashley sat still for a long time, staring at the city lights flickering through her window.

She whispered to herself, "Only a miracle can save him now."

CHAPTER 10:
THE JURY TRIAL

Monday, 9:00 A.M. Eastern District Court, Virginia

The courtroom was packed. Journalists, family members, and military observers filled every bench. The air was thick with anticipation and quiet tension.

Aadil sat beside Ashley at the defense table, his hands clasped tightly, eyes closed in silent prayer. Ashley glanced at him, her heart racing yet steady with hope.

Across the room, the District Attorney stood ready with his files. His expression was confident, almost triumphant. He had been waiting for this moment, to deliver his opening argument and demand the harshest punishment under the law.

The district judge entered, followed by three senior judges appointed as the special jury for the case, a rare arrangement reserved for war crimes and terrorism trials. The entire courtroom rose. When they sat again, the judge's calm but unreadable face commanded absolute attention.

The prosecutor rose deliberately from his seat, buttoned his dark suit jacket, and walked to the center of the courtroom floor. His steps echoed against the polished marble as the room fell into a heavy silence. His tone was firm, loud, and meticulously calculated, every word chosen to pierce through the defense.

He addressed the court, calling the case one of the most horrific chapters in American history, the terrorist attacks of September 11, 2001, that claimed nearly three thousand innocent lives. He spoke of Tora Bora, of proximity, of silence, and of guilt. He described Aadil Gul not as a bystander but as a willing accomplice, a trusted aide to Osama bin Laden.

Then he introduced the new accusation, his voice sharpening as he described an alleged ambush. He claimed that when General Hughes and his men attempted to apprehend Aadil, he turned violent, seized a weapon, fired on American troops, killed one soldier, and wounded the general himself.

Gasps rippled through the gallery. Ashley's heart clenched as she looked instinctively toward Aadil. He sat motionless, jaw tight, staring straight ahead.

The prosecutor let the tension stretch before concluding. He declared that this was no misunderstanding, no coincidence, but treason, and for crimes so grave, there could be only one just punishment: death without parole.

He returned to his table, hands clasped behind him, eyes cold with certainty.

The courtroom fell into utter stillness, broken only by the faint clicking of camera shutters. Ashley leaned slightly toward Aadil and whispered for him to stay calm. Let him finish.

Yet deep down, she felt the chill of fear. This time, she knew, the fight would take a miracle.

When the lead judge nodded and invited the defense to proceed, Ashley stood. She adjusted her notes, her hands steady despite the storm inside her chest.

She began by acknowledging the pain of September 11, the grief every American carried, including herself. She spoke of memory, fear, and loss, but reminded the court that grief could never replace truth, and justice could not exist in the shadow of assumption or revenge.

She described Aadil not as a terrorist or a soldier of hatred, but as a man, a husband, a son, a U.S. citizen who had been trapped by war, deception, and fear. She challenged the idea that geography defined guilt, asking whether a man running into a burning building to save a friend should be called an arsonist.

She laid out a different story, one stripped of drama and prejudice. A story of a man who traveled to Pakistan to visit family and tried to rescue a kidnapped friend near the Afghan border, only to be captured himself, beaten, and mislabeled by those desperate to claim a victory.

For years, she said, he had been silenced and locked away not by proof, but by perception. Today, for the first time, he had a voice.

She made it clear she was not fighting America, but defending the principles that defined it: fairness, truth, and the courage to confront error. She asked the judges to listen with both mind and conscience, because justice rested not on anger or fear, but on courage.

When she finished, the room was quiet.

The lead judge leaned forward and asked whether the government had its witnesses.

For the first time, the prosecutor hesitated. He adjusted his tie, shuffled papers, and said the witnesses were on their way. He turned sharply toward his assistant, who whispered that they had no signal, no confirmation. The convoy had left the base at dawn.

A murmur spread through the courtroom. Journalists leaned forward. The three senior judges exchanged uneasy glances.

Ashley felt her pulse racing. Her hands trembled beneath the table. Across the aisle, the prosecutor's composure began to unravel.

In the second row, General Robert sat motionless, his phone resting quietly on his knee, his expression unreadable. Ashley noticed the stillness, the calm, and felt a knot tighten in her stomach.

When the judge announced an early lunch recess, the gavel echoed sharply through the room.

Ashley leaned toward Aadil and whispered for him to stay calm and not react to anything. He nodded, his eyes full of fear and trust.

As the courtroom emptied, Ashley glanced once more at her uncle. He had not moved. His phone screen remained dark, but his eyes told her something had already begun.

At one o'clock sharp, the bailiff called the court back to order. The judges re-entered, and the tension in the room thickened. The prosecutor's table was still half-empty. His assistants whispered urgently into their phones.

The lead judge asked again whether the witness had arrived.

The prosecutor admitted they had been unable to reach General Hughes or any member of his unit.

The murmurs grew louder.

Then the courtroom door opened.

A young court clerk hurried in, pale and breathless, carrying a sealed envelope marked with a red crest reserved for classified communications. The judge accepted it and broke the seal. As he read, his expression changed. He folded the paper carefully and looked up.

He announced that the court had received a classified directive from the Department of Defense and the Department of Justice. The charges against Aadil Gul had been re-evaluated based on newly verified intelligence. General Hughes and members of his unit were now under federal investigation. There was no legal basis to proceed.

The courtroom erupted.

The judge raised his hand and declared the case dismissed, effective immediately. Aadil Gul was free to go.

Ashley covered her mouth as tears streamed down her face. Aadil stood frozen, disbelief etched into every line of his body. The prosecutor sank into his chair, papers slipping from his hands.

The gavel struck again. Court adjourned.

As the bailiffs opened the gate, Ashley ran to Aadil. Their embrace was silent, desperate, and real.

At the back of the courtroom, General Robert rose quietly. He lifted his phone, murmured a few words, and turned toward the exit. Ashley caught his eye for just a second. He gave her a slight nod, then disappeared into the corridor.

Through her tears, she mouthed thank you.

Outside, sunlight broke through the clouds and spilled across the courthouse steps. Aadil inhaled deeply, the air of freedom clean and unfamiliar. Ashley slipped her hand into his.

"It's over," she whispered.

Together, they stepped into the light.

And deep in her heart, Ashley knew this had been more than a court victory. It was a quiet war, won in the shadows.

CHAPTER 11: REAL TEST

Ashley looked at her uncle, her voice filled with relief. She told him they wanted to thank him personally. She admitted she had truly believed they were going to lose the case and that his strategy had worked when nothing else seemed possible. Words, she said, were not enough to express their gratitude.

General Robert told them they were welcome and that he was glad that part was finally over. He added that he appreciated how carefully Ashley had followed his directions.

Aadil asked what the next step would be.

General Robert explained that he would arrange a high-level meeting with senior Pentagon officials, including the Joint Chiefs of Staff and the Director of the CIA. That meeting, he said, would be Aadil's real test. He would need to prove his abilities there.

Ashley asked directly what the actual deal had been between him and the officials, admitting she knew he had met with both the Joint Chiefs and the CIA Director.

General Robert answered honestly. He said he had told them everything about Aadil's background: his time with the ISI, his work as a bodyguard for Bin Laden's assistant, Sheikh Mohammed, and his advanced military training. He explained how deeply familiar Aadil was with the mountainous regions of Afghanistan and northern Pakistan. He told them he had given his personal guarantee, a gamble by any standard, that Aadil could help track Bin Laden's whereabouts.

Their only concern, he said, had been trust. Could they rely on Aadil? General Robert had assured them they could.

He looked at Ashley gently and reminded her that her father, David, had been his closest friend and that she was like family to him. He said he could not bear to see her lose the case, and so he had taken the risk. Now, he added quietly, he hoped Aadil would not let him down.

That night, in a secure conference room deep inside the Pentagon, the atmosphere was tense. Aadil sat across from the Joint Chiefs of Staff and the Director of the CIA, with General Robert beside him. The room was dimly lit, the low hum of surveillance equipment filling the silence.

The CIA Director asked Aadil to give his full background, everything from the day he was born.

What Aadil did not see was the team of psychologists and behavioral analysts seated behind a one-way mirror in an adjoining room. Hidden cameras and biometric sensors recorded every movement, every hesitation, every shift in his voice. Their job was to determine whether he was telling the truth and whether he could be trusted.

The questioning lasted half an hour. They covered his work with the ISI, his training, his role as a bodyguard to Sheikh Mohammed, and his years moving through the border regions of Afghanistan and northern Pakistan.

Aadil had expected this. As a former intelligence operative, he understood the psychological tests. General Robert had warned him in advance that they would push him to his limits and that the only option was to tell the truth, every detail.

When the evaluation ended, a silent signal came from the observation room. The experts had cleared him. He was truthful, and his intentions appeared genuine.

The CIA Director acknowledged the result and said they had already done extensive work trying to locate Bin Laden, with little success. He explained that they had a local contact, Dr. Shahid Afridi, a physician working undercover, who would assist Aadil on the ground.

He leaned forward and told Aadil that the mission was simple in theory but deadly in execution. He needed to find Bin Laden. Whether he was hiding across the Afghan border or deep inside Pakistan, they needed confirmation. It would be a long and dangerous mission, with no margin for error.

Aadil nodded silently, aware that his real test had only just begun.

Later, in the same steel-gray conference room during the day, fluorescent lights humming overhead, Aadil sat beside Ashley. Across from them, the Joint Chiefs of Staff and the CIA Director reviewed files marked Top Secret, Eyes Only.

Aadil asked to make one request before they began. He said his wife knew everything about his past and about the mission. He did not want to lie to her again. He explained that Ashley wanted to join him.

The officials exchanged glances. The Joint Chiefs noted that such missions were classified at the highest level.

Ashley spoke calmly, saying she understood the risk and was not there as a tourist. Whatever Aadil faced, she would face too.

The CIA Director leaned forward and said that if they allowed this, their identities would have to be airtight. They would have to live their cover completely. No one, not family, not friends, not embassy staff, could know.

He slid a sealed dossier across the table. It outlined a cover with the G Foundation, a vaccination program. Dr. Afridi would lead a legitimate immunization initiative, and Ashley and Aadil would join as field officers monitoring child vaccinations.

The Joint Chiefs explained that this would be their public role. Their real assignment would be to intercept local communications, phone chatter, radio traffic, and courier routes, all feeding into encrypted systems.

The CIA Director added that they would work with Dr. Afridi in the northern territories. The mission could take a year or much longer. There was no timeline, only the objective.

Aadil agreed but said he did not want Ashley's life to be in danger.

Ashley interrupted softly, saying she was already committed. Her life without him, she said, had already ended once. She would not let it happen again.

The room fell silent. The officials exchanged another look, the kind that sealed decisions.

The Joint Chiefs told them that if they succeeded, they would be rewarded accordingly. The bounty would be significant. Their training would begin in sixty days, followed by deployment.

Aadil made one final request. When they arrived in Pakistan, he wanted to visit his family and spend at least a week with his mother.

The CIA Director agreed, on the condition that there be no discussion of the mission. To everyone there, they would be employees helping vaccinate children.

Both Aadil and Ashley agreed.

They were told they would receive identification, specialized phones, and monitoring devices disguised as medical tools. Everything would need to be hidden carefully.

The officials stood, signaling the end of the meeting. They said they would be in touch when it was time for the next phase.

Aadil and Ashley rose, exchanged brief salutes, and walked out together. Their footsteps echoed down the long metallic hallway, heavy with the weight of their new reality.

Aadil told Ashley that although they had promised to live together, he hated that she was sacrificing her law career for him. He said she had proven she was an incredible attorney and could succeed anywhere.

Ashley smiled faintly and told him that family mattered more to her than any courtroom. He was her life. After the mission, she said, maybe she would return to law, maybe not. For now, she just wanted them to be together.

She took his hand and told him she had fought destiny once to bring him back and would not lose him again. Wherever they lived, his mother would live with them too.

Aadil, deeply moved, told her she had given him everything he never deserved and that he would never forget it. He kissed her hands, and they shared a quiet moment bound by duty, love, and secrets.

Later, Ashley hugged her mother goodbye. Tears glistened, but nothing was said about the mission.

She told her mother it was classified and that she could not tell anyone, not even her late father's old friends.

Her mother smiled softly and said she had lived her whole life keeping secrets. This one would stay locked with her.

They embraced, both aware of the unspoken risks ahead and of how much had already been placed on the line.

CHAPTER 12:
EIGHT WEEKS LATER

Dim lights. Satellite feeds flicker across the walls. The CIA Director stands before a large digital map of Pakistan, where glowing dots mark Khyber Pakhtunkhwa and Baluchistan. Across the table sit Aadil, Ashley, and General Robert.

The CIA Director said there had been a change in operational cover. The Pentagon, he explained, had decided not to attach them to the G Foundation. Instead, they would both operate under the United Nations umbrella.

Ashley looked confused, but kept her voice calm as she asked why the switch.

The CIA Director explained that under U.N. status, no government could detain them easily. Humanitarian personnel were protected under international law. They would represent the U.N. Polio Eradication Initiative, funded by the G Foundation but run through U.N. channels. Officially, both of them would be field vaccination officers responding to health emergencies in crisis zones, including floods, earthquakes, and polio outbreaks in Khyber Pakhtunkhwa and Baluchistan.

Aadil nodded slowly and said it was smart. The ISI would not suspect anything. A U.N. cover looked clean.

General Robert agreed. They would have diplomatic protection, medical paperwork, and all the permits they needed. But he reminded them that their real mission had not changed. They were still expected to intercept communication signals, locate patterns, and trace any leads on Bin Laden's network.

A couple of months of extensive training followed under joint U.N. and CIA command.

Ashley, wearing a blue vest marked "UNICEF / Polio Aid," practiced field vaccination procedures on child mannequins. Aadil ran tactical drills through desert terrain, switching between radios, handling encrypted equipment, and assembling portable tracking devices. In classroom briefings, they studied regional dialects, cultural behavior, medical ethics, and cover maintenance. Together, Aadil and Ashley injected training serums into mock patients, their teamwork flawless.

General Robert reminded them that the humanitarian mission was real. They would vaccinate hundreds of children, and that would be their legitimacy. The intelligence part had to remain invisible.

One evening, Aadil and Ashley sat together on the porch steps, sweat still on their faces from drills. The sun bled red over the horizon.

Ashley admitted the military part was more complex than she had expected. She laughed and told Aadil he moved like he had done it a thousand times.

Aadil smiled faintly and said he had. ISI training never left you. But this time, he added, the cause felt cleaner. He paused and told her she was good with the vaccination teams and that they believed her instantly.

Ashley said that was the easy part, because mothers trusted sincerity. It was the secret that worried her.

They sat in silence for a moment.

Later, the CIA Director reviewed their final deployment plan. He told them Dr. Shahid Afridi would be their ground contact. He would deliver the high-frequency trackers, encrypted phones, and other communications gear once they were settled in the north. They would carry nothing suspicious through customs.

Ashley said that was a relief, because she had been worried about security checks at Islamabad Airport.

The CIA Director told her they had thought of that. Their luggage would match that of real medical workers, with vaccines, records, and equipment. The devices would reach them later through a secure handoff.

General Robert added that their cover was airtight. He said Ashley's mother living with them would help, because no one suspected a family household. The ISI would not even blink.

A large digital map glowed on the wall, showing Afghanistan and northern Pakistan in muted satellite colors. Red circles marked Tora Bora, Peshawar, Abbottabad, and Haripur.

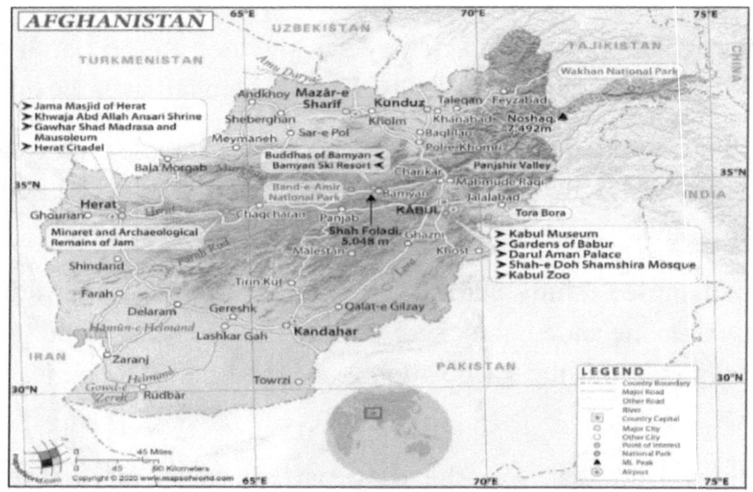

Tora Bora lies in eastern Afghanistan, within the Safed Koh mountain range, also known as the White Mountains, near the border with Pakistan. It is situated in the Pachir Aw Agam District of Nangarhar Province, approximately fifty kilometers west of the Khyber Pass. Jalalabad lies about thirty kilometers to the northwest, making the region a critical corridor between Afghanistan and Pakistan.

Around the table sat Aadil, General Robert, General Harrison of the Joint Chiefs of Staff, and CIA Director Morgan. The room hummed with tension and quiet calculation, every man aware that the decisions made here could alter history.

Director Morgan broke the silence. He said their analysts still believed remnants of bin Laden's network stretched from Jalalabad across the border into Pakistan. The real question, he added, was where exactly they should place Aadil on the ground.

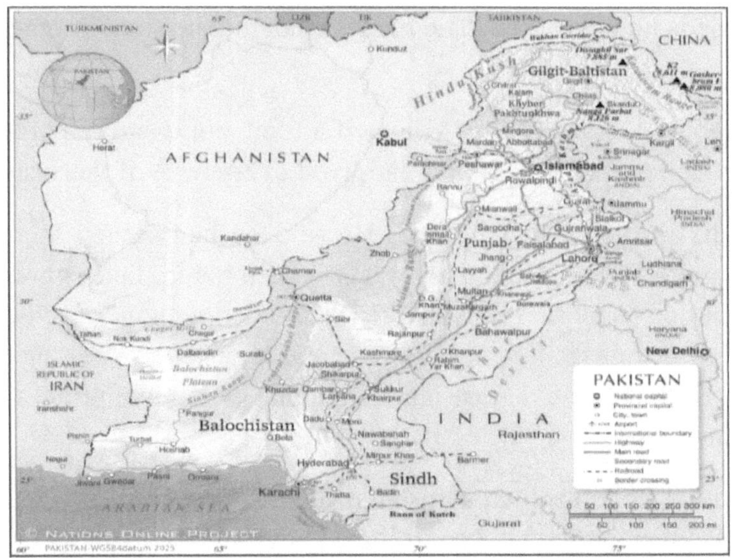

The northern part of Pakistan, including Abbottabad, is characterized by dramatic mountain ranges such as the Himalayas, Karakoram, and Hindu Kush, which converge in the region. Abbottabad lies in the east central part of Khyber Pakhtunkhwa Province, situated on a plateau at the southern edge of the Rash (Orash) Plain, near the foothills of the Himalayas. Major towns in this broader area include Mansehra, Gilgit, and Karimabad.

Aadil leaned over the table and pointed at the map. He said they should start there, explaining that the corridor between Tora Bora and Abbottabad, with its ridges and deep valleys, was a world of its own. Few outsiders went in, and even the ISI avoided certain zones at night.

He traced his finger eastward toward Haripur and continued that if they set their base there, they would be close enough to the frontier for movement and far enough from the tribal hotspots. It sat halfway between the plains and the mountains, making it perfect cover for a humanitarian team.

General Harrison leaned forward and asked if Haripur was about forty kilometers from Abbottabad.

Aadil replied that it was forty, maybe forty-five. He added that there were plenty of routes north toward Mansehra and the border belts, roads he knew well. The names changed, he said, but the habits did not.

Director Morgan allowed himself a faint smile and remarked that Aadil sounded like a man who had lived every mile of that map.

Aadil answered that he had. He said he had served there once under another flag, and that locals remembered faces more than allegiances. His mother lived in the Hazara region, which would make their presence natural. A foreign wife and a local son working for the United Nations would raise no suspicion, as humanitarian aid was rarely questioned.

General Robert said that this aligned with the new directive. Under the U.N. cover, they would coordinate with Dr. Afridi out of Peshawar. All field data would be encrypted before upload, with no American signatures anywhere in the chain.

General Harrison added that they could provide satellite reconnaissance over the Haripur to Abbottabad corridor every seventy-two hours. Aadil would flag anything unusual, and they would triangulate from space.

Director Morgan reminded him that the first objective was not confrontation but confirmation. He told him to verify movement, identify communication patterns, and remain invisible.

Aadil nodded and said he understood. Haripur offered proximity, safety, and a sense of identity. That was where they would start.

Silence settled over the room. Then Director Morgan nodded in agreement and said that Haripur it was. Operation Blue Crescent would begin in thirty days.

On the screen, the map zoomed in on Haripur, a valley town wrapped in green hills, a crossroads between the plains and the northern mountains. A red marker began to blink steadily.

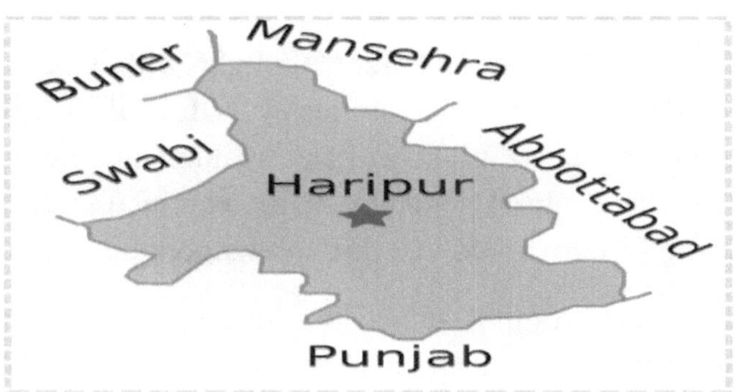

Haripur was a place where the mountains seemed to whisper secrets, where every echo could be the sound of a ghost returning.

Aadil looked at General Robert with quiet gratitude and said that it made things easier. He added that his mother had always been his strength.

A U.N. aircraft waited on the tarmac, white and blue beneath the rising sun. Workers moved efficiently around it, loading crates clearly marked "HUMANITARIAN AID, POLIO RESPONSE."

Aadil and Ashley walked toward the plane wearing official U.N. identification badges, their expressions calm but focused. From a distance, General Robert watched them go.

He thought that they would be the most important couple no one would ever hear about.

They glanced at each other and intertwined their fingers.

Ashley asked if he was ready.

Aadil replied that he was always ready for the mission. As for what came after, he said he would take it one sunrise at a time.

They boarded the plane. The engines roared, and the aircraft began its slow roll toward the runway.

CHAPTER 13: THE SETUP IN HARIPUR

The city glowed in the hazy mountain light, with wide boulevards, trimmed hedges, and army checkpoints every few blocks. Behind tall walls and barbed gates sat a quiet gated residential colony, home to senior officers and retired generals. At the entrance, security guards waved a white UNO-marked van through without hesitation.

Inside the van, Aadil watched the houses roll past, manicured lawns, flags, and armed sentries blending into one another. Beside him, Ashley clutched a small duffel and a folder of paperwork. At the wheel was Saleem, a local driver wearing a UNO badge.

Saleem told them that Dr. Afridi sent his regards and said their villa was ready.

Ashley looked out the window and remarked that it did not look like the field.

"That's the point," Aadil replied quietly. "Among generals, nobody suspects spies."

The villa was small but elegant, a three-bedroom house tucked near a row of government bungalows. Blue UNO decals marked the gate, and a discreet guard post stood by the wall. Saleem unloaded their luggage and explained that he would return in two days. Until then, they would remain settled before driving to the UNO office in Islamabad to meet Dr. Afridi.

Inside, the house was simple and clean, with white tiles, ceiling fans, and a modest sitting room. One bedroom was set aside for Aadil and Ashley, another prepared carefully for Aadil's mother, and the third furnished as an office with a steel cabinet and two desks.

Later, when they finally sat with their family, Aadil and Ashley kept their tone casual and hopeful. There could be no mention of the CIA, the Pentagon, or the risks ahead, only the humanitarian story they had been instructed to tell.

Aadil poured tea for everyone and explained that they had both been hired by the United Nations for a public health program. Their job, he said, would be to help parents understand the importance of polio vaccination for their children.

His mother's face brightened. She asked if that meant they would be helping sick children.

Ashley smiled and said yes. With the help of the UNO and the G Foundation, the world was almost free from polio. It had been eliminated in more than ninety-nine percent of countries, with only a few pockets remaining, mostly in Pakistan, Afghanistan, and remote border regions.

Aadil continued, explaining that in Pakistan, especially in the North West Frontier Province and Baluchistan, some parents still refused the vaccine. Many believed old myths that the drops were unsafe or against their faith. Others were simply unaware, or too poor to reach medical centers.

Leaning forward, he spoke with conviction. Their job would be to change that, to go village by village, speak with local leaders, convince families, and make sure no child was left unprotected. Polio, he said, was cruel. It paralyzed for life. There was no cure and no recovery. Just one drop could prevent it.

Ashley added that the G Foundation funded most of the vaccination drives in partnership with the World Health Organization, UNICEF, and Pakistan's Ministry of Health. Thousands of health workers had been trained, especially women, to reach families even in the most remote mountain regions.

Aadil's mother looked at them with pride and said it was good work, that they would be saving lives.

Aadil nodded, forcing a calm smile. Deep inside, he knew their mission was far more complex. Behind the syringes and vaccine boxes lay layers of intelligence, secrecy, and danger.

But to his family, and to the world, they were now humanitarian workers, the face of compassion in a land where suspicion had long replaced trust.

CHAPTER 14:
THE BRIEFING AT THE UNO OFFICE

After a few days of rest at their house in Haripur, Ashley and Aadil reported to the United Nations field operations office, the first official step of their new assignment. The staff had been briefed about their arrival. Their credentials, identification cards, and crisp new uniforms waited on a polished desk, along with a map outlining their assigned working territory.

Outside, a white UNO van gleamed under the sun. To anyone else, it looked like an ordinary field vehicle used for aid deliveries. But this one was special, armored and bullet resistant, its interior discreetly fitted with the latest communications suite: encrypted radio, satellite uplink, and a digital navigation system calibrated for the rugged terrain of northern Pakistan.

Their duty station would be a small UNO sub-branch in Haripur, roughly a hundred miles north of Islamabad. They were scheduled to begin work the following Monday.

That afternoon, they met Dr. Shahid Afridi, the man tasked with coordinating medical logistics. He explained to Aadil and Ashley the security and political situation facing polio workers in the region.

Ashley asked why some areas were resistant to polio vaccination.

Dr. Afridi explained that while most of Pakistan supported vaccination, specific communities in the North West Frontier Province and parts of Baluchistan had shown strong resistance to polio campaigns. The reasons, he said, were deeply layered, shaped by history, social structures, and politics.

Over the decades, these regions had experienced conflict and intelligence operations that created deep mistrust toward foreign organizations, including the United Nations and Western NGOs. In addition, certain extremist groups and local clerics had spread false rumors that polio vaccines were un-Islamic or caused infertility. These misconceptions were often amplified through local sermons, pamphlets, and social media, convincing some parents that the vaccines were part of a Western plot.

In many rural areas, literacy rates were low, and access to credible health information was limited. Families who had never seen a doctor or modern medicine were easily influenced by fear and misinformation. Security and political instability also played a role. Many parts of the North West Frontier Province and Baluchistan were volatile, with militant activity, tribal conflicts, and a weak government presence. Health workers traveling door to door were often viewed with suspicion. Tragically, over the years, hundreds of polio workers, primarily women, had been attacked, kidnapped, or killed by militants who accused them of being foreign agents.

Because of this resistance, Dr. Afridi explained, Pakistan remained one of only two countries in the world, along with Afghanistan, where polio was still endemic. Despite these challenges, the Pakistani government, the World Health Organization, UNICEF, and the G Foundation continued to fund and protect vaccination teams, often working with local community leaders and religious scholars to rebuild trust.

Dr. Afridi then asked if they had any plans in mind.

Aadil replied that he was already familiar with most of the area, though it had been a long time. He wanted to visit the region with Ashley and monitor the security situation firsthand. He requested one month to explore a hundred-mile radius around the Haripur UNO office. He would act as the local driver, while Ashley would accompany him as a UNO expert. After a month of observation and close monitoring, he said, he would be ready to receive the devices. If an ISI inspection of their van was required, it could be conducted at the beginning.

Dr. Afridi nodded and agreed that it was good planning.

He then produced a small leather briefcase and placed it on the table between them. Inside lay neatly stacked bundles of U.S. dollars.

Ten thousand U.S. dollars in cash for each of you, he said. Your living expenses for now. Another ten thousand in cash every month, during our meeting at my secret office. Your cover remains strictly humanitarian, vaccination, field coordination, and public health reports. Nothing more.

Aadil nodded, his face unreadable. Years of intelligence work had taught him not to show emotion, but he felt the weight of what this truly meant.

When he rejoined Ashley upstairs, she looked at him with quiet determination. They both understood the unspoken truth. Their mission had just begun, and from this moment forward, every move would count.

Aadil took the van and asked Saleem, the van driver, to work with the other workers and give them a ride.

CHAPTER 15:
SETTLING IN HARIPUR

Yasser and his family visited Aadil and Ashley at their new house. The villa, neat and bright within a secure gated community, impressed everyone. They admired the quiet neighborhood and congratulated the couple on their new UNO assignment.

That weekend, Yasser's family stayed overnight. Laughter filled the house again, children running through the hallways, Aadil's mother smiling, relaxed, and happy. On Sunday morning, before leaving for their village, Yasser promised to visit often so their mother would not feel lonely.

Every night, Ashley gently massaged Aadil's mother's hands and shoulders before bed. The old woman often whispered blessings in Urdu, calling Ashley her daughter, not her daughter-in-law.

On Monday, Aadil and Ashley reported to the local UNO Polio Coordination Office in Haripur. The office was modest but well-equipped. They met their team: two Lady Health Visitors, a secretary, a driver, and two security guards.

Aadil, familiar with the local terrain, drove and acted as a guide, arranging meetings with doctors, hospitals, and schools. Ashley, representing UNO, supervised fieldwork, oversaw data collection, and ensured each campaign was documented correctly. Every team member reported to Ashley, and Ashley reported directly to Dr. Afridi.

They outlined their one hundred-mile operational radius north, south, east, and west of Haripur, dividing the territory into weekly zones. They planned to visit every clinic, hospital, pharmacy, Basic Health Unit, Rural Health Center, and school, distributing UNO brochures and polio awareness videos.

The more visible they became, the safer their cover. The UNO logo on their van soon became a familiar sight, even at ISI checkpoints. Occasionally, the van was inspected, but the team had nothing to hide, at least for now.

They worked Monday through Thursday, leaving early in the morning and returning before dark. Friday was the official holiday, and nights were avoided for safety. Roads near the Afghan border were lined with military checkpoints, but Aadil, drawing on his experience, navigated them smoothly.

At home, Aadil's mother often sat alone during the day, her rosary beads slowly turning between her fingers. She never complained, but Aadil sensed her loneliness.

He spoke with Yasser and proposed a solution. Yasser would pick up their mother every Monday morning and bring her back to Haripur on Friday. That way, she could spend weekdays with her grandchildren and weekends with Aadil and Ashley. Everyone loved the plan.

When Yasser teased her, asking if she loved Ashley more than him or Aadil now, she smiled and replied softly that whatever Ashley had done for her son and their family, no one else could have done.

Ashley laughed, hugged her tightly, and kissed her hands.

Within a month of tireless work, Ashley and Aadil had distributed hundreds of brochures and awareness kits across Haripur district to clinics, pharmacies, Basic Health Units, Rural Health Centers, hospitals, and primary schools. Their UNO van became a familiar presence in every town and village.

Everyone saw them as the kind, dedicated polio team. No one suspected that beneath the humanitarian mission, another, far more secret operation was quietly taking shape.

CHAPTER 16:
THE FIFTH WEEK – UNDER COVER

Aadil had a natural gift, the art of communication. He spoke Pashto and Urdu fluently, with a respectful, warm tone. He knew exactly how to talk to villagers, tribal elders, and even checkpoint soldiers.

He had grown a thick beard, something that helped him blend in perfectly. In these regions, men without beards often faced suspicion. With the beard, he looked like one of them. Even Ashley adapted easily, dressing in traditional Pakistani clothes, her head always covered with a dupatta. Locals respected her modesty and began calling her "Madam Ashia," a name that sounded familiar to them.

The beard did not just change Aadil's appearance. It protected him. After ten years, and with his altered look, no one could have recognized him, not even the ISI.

Within a month, word spread across the region about the new UNO polio vaccination team. Their white van with the bold blue UNO logo became a symbol of trust. Every military and ISI checkpoint now recognized it. Their reputation grew quickly. People waved as they passed. Soldiers at checkpoints saluted and let them through without question.

It was precisely what they wanted: visibility for the mission and invisibility for the truth behind it.

Behind the public health work, however, they were waiting. Waiting for the fundamental tools of their assignment. The high-frequency voice recognition and call tracking devices had not yet arrived. In the meantime, Aadil and Ashley continued exploring the terrain, venturing off the main highways onto dusty, unpaved village roads, studying landscapes, valleys, and hidden routes.

Aadil had already identified secret places to hide the future devices: under bridges, inside broken walls, near water tanks, and at bus stops where local calls were frequently made.

In the fifth week, Ashley received a call from the UNO headquarters in Islamabad. They were requested to report in person the next morning.

The couple left Haripur early for Islamabad. The ride was quiet. Both knew something important was about to happen.

When they entered the UNO building, they were led to a restricted area, one they had not seen before. Waiting for them was Dr. Afridi, smiling as always, but this time with a hint of excitement.

He congratulated them and told them that the CIA was very pleased with their performance.

Ashley looked surprised and asked how they knew what they had been doing.

Dr. Afridi smiled faintly and explained that they had been watching them. Their UNO van was not an ordinary one. It was fitted with a satellite communication system and an advanced tracking module. Every movement, every conversation, every stop was recorded and transmitted in real time to the monitoring center.

Ashley and Aadil exchanged a silent look. They realized that their every step had been observed, not just by locals or the ISI, but by the very agency that had sent them there.

Dr. Afridi leaned closer, lowering his voice, and told them there was something else they needed to know.

He opened a digital map on one of the large monitors. Tiny red dots blinked across the northern belt of Pakistan.

DR. NAEEM MEO

Turkmenistan
Tajikistan
China
Uzbekistan
HINDU KUSH
Northern Areas
K2
© WorldAtlas.com
Kabul River
200 mi
Kabul
Khyber Pass
Jammu and Kashmir
200 km
Peshawar
Islamabad
Afghanistan
Indus River
Gujrat
Lahore
Hazarganji Chiltan N.P.
Zhob
Chenab River
PUNJAB
Quetta
Multan
N
Nok Kundi
Bahawalpur
Balochistan Plateau
Pakistan
Iran
Mashkai River
Kirthar N.P.
Sukkur
Delhi
Hingol N.P.
SINDH
Indus River
India
Gwadar
Ormara
Hyderabad
Karachi
Arabian Sea
Mouths of the Indus
PAKISTAN
TROPIC OF CANCER
LOW / HILLS / MOUNTAINS

KUWAIT
PAKISTAN
NEPAL
SAUDI ARABIA
BAHRAIN
QATAR
UNITED ARAB EMIRATES
INDIA
BANGLA
OMAN
YEMEN
ETHIOPIA
SOMALIA
SRI LANKA
MALDIVES
Bay of Be
KENYA
Red Sea

Iraq
Afghanistan
Iran
Kuwait
Strait of Hormuz
Pakistan
India
Bahrain
Qatar
Gulf of Oman
Karachi
350 m
U.A.E.
350 km
Saudi Arabia
Oman
Gulf of Kutch
Surat
Dugm
Gulf of Khambhat
Mumbai (Bombay)
Yemen
Mirbat
Qishn
Arabian Sea
India
Gulf of Aden
Suqutra (Yemen)
Laccadive Sea
Cochin
Somalia
Cape Guardafui
Lakshadweep (India)
Cape Kanyakumari
Bay of Bengal
Indian Ocean
Maldives
© WorldAtlas.com

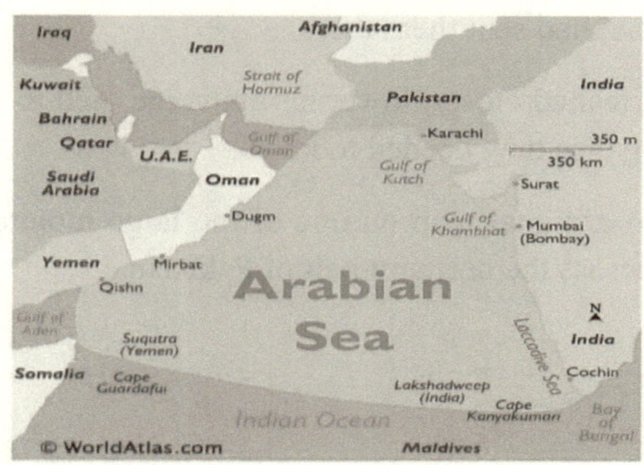

"These," he said, pointing to the screen, "are your recorded travel routes. Every stop. Every meeting. Every movement within a one-hundred-mile radius."

Ashley looked at him, confused. "But how? We didn't transmit anything manually."

Dr. Afridi smiled faintly. "You didn't have to. The system is live."

He zoomed the map outward. The satellite image expanded over Pakistan and then over the Arabian Sea. He pointed to a single blinking blue mark in the ocean.

"That," he said, "is your command center."

Aadil squinted at the screen. "A ship?"

"Yes," Afridi nodded. "A U.S. Navy warship stationed in the northern Arabian Sea. It's a floating satellite office, part of a larger surveillance grid. The team onboard monitors every field operative within this mission, including both of you. They track your van through satellite feeds, analyze your voice patterns, and store every report in encrypted military servers."

Ashley's eyes widened slightly. "So they can see us at all times?"

"Exactly," Dr. Afridi replied. "You're never alone out there. Think of it as protection and control. They know every village you entered and every checkpoint you cross. Even your conversations inside the van are automatically logged and analyzed through AI-assisted voice recognition."

Aadil nodded slowly. He understood what that meant. There would be no mistakes, no secrets, and no second chances.

Dr. Afridi continued, explaining that this level of surveillance was standard for missions of this magnitude. The Americans no longer relied on chance. They relied on data.

Ashley looked at Aadil and whispered, half to herself, "Then we're not just part of a mission. We're part of their system."

During and after the U.S.-led war in Afghanistan following 9/11, the U.S. Navy and allied forces maintained a continuous presence in the northern Arabian Sea. This included waters off the coast of Pakistan and Oman, as well as the Gulf of Oman near the Strait of Hormuz, a strategic route for Middle Eastern oil and military logistics. These waters fell under the operational authority of the U.S. Fifth Fleet, headquartered in Bahrain, and U.S. Central Command Naval Forces.

From the Arabian Sea, U.S. and NATO naval assets supported air operations into Afghanistan via aircraft carriers, monitored regional activity across Pakistan, Iran, and the Arabian Peninsula, conducted intelligence, surveillance, and reconnaissance missions, and secured sea lines of communication and logistics routes for military supplies. During the height of the Afghan war, aircraft carriers such as the USS Theodore Roosevelt, USS Abraham Lincoln, and USS Carl Vinson operated from this region to launch strike aircraft into Afghanistan and Pakistan.

Dr. Afridi closed the office door behind them and walked toward a large painting on the wall, a landscape of Islamabad's Parliament House. With a quiet click, he pressed a small remote on his keychain. The painting slid aside, revealing a hidden steel door.

Ashley's eyes widened. "What is this place?"

Afridi smiled faintly. "Our real office."

He led them inside. The room was large and cold, filled with glowing monitors, receivers, and racks of encrypted servers. Multiple satellite feeds flickered on the walls, displaying real-time data such as coordinates, signal strengths, and intercepted transmissions.

"This," Afridi said, "is the CIA's secondary communication center, operating under the UNO cover. Every conversation within a twenty-mile radius of Islamabad's government buildings passes through here."

Ashley looked around in shock. "You mean you're recording the politicians?"

"Not just politicians," Afridi replied calmly. "Army officers, intelligence officers, even the prime minister, the foreign minister, the president, or members of Parliament. Anyone who matters."

He pointed to a digital map of Pakistan on the screen and explained that the building was less than a mile from Parliament House. Another facility operated beside the GHQ in Rawalpindi, and both were linked to the U.S. satellite office aboard the naval ship in the northern Arabian Sea.

Ashley was speechless.

Aadil, however, stood quietly, his expression steady. He had seen this kind of operation before. He knew how the ISI used similar tactics, high-frequency recorders sourced from China and Russia, planted near ministries, courts, and tax offices. It was all about leverage and control.

Ashley turned to Dr. Afridi. "Why would the Pakistani Army and ISI spy on their own people?"

Afridi sighed. "Because that's how power works here. Information is control. Every minister, judge, or bureaucrat has secrets, and whoever owns those secrets controls the country."

Dr. Afridi opened another locked cabinet and pulled out a small black box. Inside were hundreds of miniature tracking devices, each no larger than a cigarette lighter.

"These," he said, "are high-frequency, long-range intercept units. Each one can monitor phone calls and radio transmissions within a radius of five to twenty miles. Once activated, the signal links directly to the U.S. Navy's satellite network."

He handed one to Aadil. "You'll hide them in key areas near markets, schools, and village communication towers. Never more than ten miles apart. Place one or two each week. No pattern, no routine."

Ashley examined one closely. "How long will they work?"

"The battery lasts five to seven years. You won't need to worry about replacements."

Aadil nodded, absorbing every word. He already had places in mind: remote mountain paths, valley mosques, and border towns where communication flowed freely but suspicion ran high.

Before leaving, Afridi unlocked a drawer and handed Aadil a specialized laptop and a pair of encrypted satellite phones.

"These are preconfigured for direct connection," he explained. "You'll message through a secure channel first, then confirm by voice. Don't ever reverse that order."

He closed the briefcase on the table and pushed it toward them. "Cash. Emergency funds. Keep it hidden. You'll need it one day."

He looked at them both seriously. "Take your time. One or two devices a week is more than enough. Be careful. ISI may have scanners. If they catch you, deny everything. You're UNO employees, nothing more."

Aadil and Ashley nodded.

"Understood," Aadil said. "We'll proceed carefully."

"And continue the vaccination work so everything looks normal," Ashley added.

"Exactly," Afridi said. "Balance both worlds. One saves lives. The other saves nations."

As they walked out, the painting slid silently back into place, erasing all trace of what they had just seen.

CHAPTER 17:
THE LOCAL UNO OFFICE –
MORNING BRIEFING

The next morning, Ashley and Aadil spent the entire day inside their local UNO branch office in Haripur. The small building buzzed with activity, nurses checking vaccine boxes, drivers preparing vehicles, and Lady Health Visitors updating charts on new households reached.

Ashley gathered the team around. "Let's have a weekly meeting every Friday," she said firmly. "We'll review progress, handle complaints, and make sure the cold chain for vaccines stays uninterrupted."

Everyone nodded. The team respected her leadership. She was disciplined but kind.

While Ashley worked with the vaccination team, Aadil sat in a small corner office surrounded by maps of the region, the northern valleys, the mountain passes, and the bordering tribal zones. He spread out a large terrain map on the table, pressing colored pushpins into key locations. Some pins marked checkpoints and communication towers, others marked remote villages and border trails.

His goal was clear: to create a perfect grid of surveillance coverage without ever arousing suspicion. The CIA had instructed him to handle one or two devices per week, but Aadil's instinct told him he could safely manage one device per day if he planned the routes carefully and used the vaccination work as cover.

That evening, as they reviewed the map together, Ashley asked quietly, "Are you sure this won't put us on ISI's radar?"

Aadil nodded. "We'll stay away from known ISI hideouts and military supply roads. Those are the danger zones. The trick is to look like we belong, like we're too ordinary to notice."

Their villa in Haripur had quickly become both home and headquarters. Dr. Afridi had chosen it himself, a modest three-bedroom house in a secure gated community where several army officers lived.

What impressed Aadil most, however, was what lay beneath it. Behind a locked door in the kitchen pantry was a stairway leading to a secret basement, a small but sophisticated space equipped with radio monitors, satellite receivers, and a direct encrypted line to the communication ship in the northern Arabian Sea.

"This house," Aadil said to Ashley as he scanned the setup, "was chosen for a reason. Afridi thinks of everything."

They agreed that once a few devices were placed, they would spend nights in the basement monitoring intercepted signals, voice samples, call frequencies, and any data that could hint at the elusive trail of Bin Laden.

Outside, the air was beginning to cool. In this region, winter hit hard. Snow often blocked roads and mountain passes for nearly four months.

Aadil pinned a final note on the wall map. "We have a window of two to three months," he said. "After that, movement will be impossible. We finish before the snow."

Ashley nodded, determination in her eyes. "Then we start tomorrow. One step at a time."

The first seven days went more smoothly than expected. Aadil and Ashley managed to implant fifteen devices across remote valleys and along dusty supply roads. Each one was carefully hidden inside old culverts, beneath utility poles, and even within the stone walls of abandoned watchtowers.

In the second week, another ten devices were placed without a single problem. The team was gaining confidence. Their cover as UNO vaccination coordinators worked perfectly. Every village they entered welcomed them, believing they were saving children from polio, which, in a way, they truly were.

By the third week, Aadil's instincts began to tingle. While driving along a narrow dirt road near the foothills, he noticed a dark green jeep following them at a distance. Each time he slowed, the jeep slowed too. When he stopped, it passed them, only to return minutes later from the opposite direction.

"Ashley," he said quietly, keeping his eyes on the mirror, "we're being followed."

She turned slightly. "ISI?"

"Most likely. They know this terrain better than anyone."

They cancelled that day's implantation plan and instead visited a few rural clinics to maintain their humanitarian cover.

The next morning, Aadil proposed going alone into the northern highlands, saying it was too dangerous for both of them. Ashley refused. "We started together. We go together."

That day, they found five strong locations, each deep in isolated valleys. But as they headed back, the same ISI jeep blocked the road. Two men stepped out, armed and alert.

"What are you doing in this restricted zone?" one demanded. "No one lives here."

Aadil kept calm and showed their UNO identification cards. "Sir, we got lost while visiting a rural clinic. We're part of the polio vaccination program."

The ISI agent studied them, then the bulletproof UNO van. After a tense silence, he handed back the IDs. "Be careful. You shouldn't be here. People get shot in these areas."

Aadil forced a polite smile. "Understood."

As they drove away, Ashley exhaled. "That was close."

"Yes," Aadil said. "Lucky they didn't check inside the van."

They were silent the rest of the way, hearts pounding but satisfied that week's mission was complete.

Days later, while trying to reach a particularly remote area, their van could go no further. The dirt track ended abruptly in the mountains.

"I'll go on foot," Aadil said, grabbing two devices. "Stay inside the van. Keep the engine running."

Ashley protested, but he was already gone.

After an hour, a figure appeared on a ridge, watching him. Aadil immediately sensed danger, undercover ISI, no doubt. He planted one device hastily near a rocky slope and began retreating.

"Stop!" the man shouted, raising his rifle. "Stop or I'll shoot!"

Aadil ran, slipping and sliding down the mountain as a shot echoed through the valley. He didn't look back.

Hours later, Ashley sat nervously in the van with headphones on, unaware of the gunfire. When Aadil finally emerged, clothes torn, face bruised, gasping for breath, she jumped up.

"Where have you been?"

"No time. Let's move."

He kept checking the rearview mirror as they sped toward the highway. "Give me that shirt from the back," he said. "I need to change before the next checkpoint."

He swapped his dusty shirt, fixed his beard and hair, and drove straight into the next military checkpoint. The guards eyed them carefully.

"Anyone suspicious in that area?"

Aadil replied smoothly in Pashto, "No, sir. We were giving polio vaccination training at the rural clinic."

They waved him through.

Once clear, they pulled over. Ashley looked at him, her voice soft but firm. "We need a break, Aadil. This is getting too dangerous."

He nodded, wiping sweat from his forehead. "We've already implanted around eighty devices. Only twenty left, and forty-five days before the snow cuts off the region."

"Then let's rest," she said. "For now, we'll focus only on the vaccination work."

Aadil smiled faintly. "Agreed."

Every night after dinner, Aadil and Ashley descended quietly into the hidden basement of their villa. The small room glowed dimly under the blue light of computer screens, their secret operations center. A large map covered one wall, dotted with red pins marking the locations of all the tracking devices.

Ashley booted up the secure CIA laptop and connected it to the encrypted satellite network. One by one, the devices lit up on the digital map, all still active and transmitting faint but steady signals.

She exhaled in relief. "All operational."

Aadil nodded. "That's good. It means no one has discovered them yet."

The only new message on the CIA terminal was short and vague: "Status check acknowledged. Thumbs up."

Ashley frowned. "When do you think we'll start seeing suspicious signals or movements?"

Aadil leaned back in his chair, rubbing his chin thoughtfully. "Not until winter. That's when things usually happen. During summer, the

CIA, the Afghan Army, the ISI, and even the Pakistani Army are all over the mountains, drones in the sky, patrols on the roads. But in winter, everything shuts down. Roads are buried under snow, and even the military pulls back. That's when the Taliban, and probably Bin Laden's network, move around freely. They know every secret pass and every hidden trail."

"So," Ashley said, "you think our real signals will come between November and March?"

"Exactly. That's our window."

She smiled softly. "Then we'll bring your mom here full-time for the winter. She'll be safer with us."

Aadil laughed quietly. "You care about my mother more than you care about me."

Ashley grinned. "Of course I do. She's easier to handle."

He chuckled. "You're lucky she loves you more than she loves me."

Ashley leaned back, a distant thought in her eyes. "I'm also thinking maybe I'll ask if my mother can visit during that time. It would be nice, two mothers under one roof."

Aadil smiled. "That would be great. She'll love it here, peaceful and quiet, even with all this madness around."

They exchanged a look, tired, hopeful, and bound by the secret they shared. Then, turning back to the screen, they spent another hour reviewing the map before shutting everything down.

The following two weeks were quieter. They focused entirely on their UNO vaccination campaign, traveling from village to village, distributing brochures, checking on clinics, and meeting with local health workers. But every night, when the valley grew silent, and the cold wind howled outside, they returned to the basement, watching the flickering map and waiting for the first suspicious signal to break the stillness.

After a two-week break, Aadil and Ashley resumed the device placement task. This time, Aadil was extra cautious. He scanned the terrain carefully, marking no-go areas and sensitive zones on the map.

"Better to place the devices just outside these restricted areas," he said to Ashley. "The high-frequency units can still cover ten to twenty-five miles. No need to take unnecessary risks."

Over the next few days, they successfully installed the remaining high-frequency, long-range phone and wireless interception devices across northern Pakistan.

If Bin Laden remained hidden in the Afghanistan border areas near Tora Bora, the devices would not pick up signals. These units were focused solely on northern Pakistan.

Ashley looked at the fully lit map one evening. "We've done it. All devices are operational."

Aadil nodded. "Only a couple of minor incidents. Nothing serious. Overall, a clean operation."

CHAPTER 18:
MEETING WITH DR. AFRIDI

A few days later, they received a secure message from Dr. Afridi requesting a meeting at the UNO Headquarters in Islamabad.

When they arrived, Afridi gestured toward a massive wall-mounted monitor displaying all the device locations.

"Well done," he said, his eyes scanning the screen. "You have the same laptops for monitoring, but my screen shows everything at once. The Navy ship satellite office has a similar setup, and experts are analyzing the phone signals around the clock."

Aadil shared the minor incidents that had occurred, and Afridi nodded.

"Good news," Afridi continued. "Your placement task is complete. You're free for the next five months. Polio vaccination fieldwork is suspended from November to April because of winter."

Ashley raised an eyebrow. "Five months off?"

Afridi smiled faintly. "Yes. But it's also safer. If the ISI is watching, it would look suspicious if UNO coordinators remain in the area during winter. Realistically, it's better for you to return to the U.S. for these months. Meanwhile, your cover remains intact."

He handed them instructions.

Lock the villa securely.

Return laptops, remaining devices, and encrypted phones in the special bag he had given them.

Leave the UNO van at the headquarters.

Aadil asked, "What about the cash?"

Afridi reassured them. "Extra cash is available at the office. You're allowed to take up to ten thousand dollars in cash into the U.S."

Aadil nodded. "Understood. Thank you."

Ashley smiled. "Five months of relative peace, finally."

Afridi's expression remained serious. "Enjoy it while you can. Winter is quiet, but come April, the real work begins."

Ashley had been quietly thinking ahead during their final days in Pakistan. Five months off meant five months of freedom and planning.

Neither she nor Aadil had yet told their mothers about the winter break. They wanted to make sure everything was settled first.

The following weekend, they visited Yasser's house. His family greeted them warmly. Over tea, Aadil explained their new schedule.

"We'll be returning to the U.S. for five months," he said. "It's part of the UNO's winter policy. We'll rejoin the field mission in April."

Yasser smiled, but his mother's eyes lit up with relief.

"That's wonderful," she said. "Ashley, you should spend time with your mother. She must miss you."

Ashley nodded. "Yes, she does. And I miss her too."

Later that evening, Aadil turned to Ashley as they packed.

"You think you might do some legal work while we're there? Maybe take a case or two?"

"I'll check with my law firm," Ashley replied thoughtfully. "If they still need help, I can handle a few clients while we're home."

That night, she called her mother, Lucy, in D.C.

"Mom, we're coming home at the end of October."

Lucy's voice trembled with excitement. "Oh, sweetheart, I can't wait to see you both. It's been too long."

Before leaving, Ashley and Aadil informed their local UNO staff in Haripur. Everyone was familiar with the seasonal rotation. Foreign staff usually leave during the harsh winters.

"We'll see you again on April first," Ashley told them with a warm smile.

Together, they double-checked the villa, especially the hidden basement, ensuring no trace of CIA equipment or activity remained. Every document, laptop, and device was accounted for and returned.

They deposited their extra cash into their Pakistani bank account and bought Aadil's mother a new Toyota Corolla as a thank-you gift. Aadil also transferred ten thousand dollars into her personal account for expenses.

"Mom deserves peace," Ashley said softly as they handed over the car keys.

"She does," Aadil agreed. "She's been through enough."

They spent their last few days shopping in Islamabad and enjoying quiet dinners with Yasser's family.

At D.C. Airport, Lucy was waiting near the arrival gate, her silver hair tucked neatly under a wool hat. She was still driving, and proud of it, at eighty years old.

"Welcome home!" she cried, rushing forward as soon as she saw them.

Ashley hugged her tightly, tears forming in her eyes.

"Mom, you still drive like a pro," she laughed.

Lucy smiled. "Of course I do. Now, let's get home. I made your favorite pie."

Back in Washington, Aadil was more excited than anyone about Ashley's plan to return to court.

"You should do it," he told her. "You're an incredible lawyer, and you miss it. The mission can wait, for now."

Ashley smiled. "It's not about the money, Aadil. I want to help people again. That's what being a public defender means to me."

They were already financially secure. The CIA and UNO contracts paid well, and both knew more bonuses would come.

The next morning, Ashley received a call from the Pentagon.

"Mrs. Ashley and Mr. Aadil, you're requested to report tomorrow morning to General Robert's office," the voice said formally.

The following day, they arrived at the Pentagon, where General Robert greeted them warmly.

"It's good to see both of you," he said, shaking their hands. "Washington's proud of your performance. You've done extraordinary work under impossible conditions."

Ashley smiled politely, while Aadil gave a firm nod.

"You'll have some time to relax now," the General continued. "Report back one week before your next deployment, at the end of March next year. Until then, enjoy your life here."

He handed two sealed envelopes to his secretary, who passed them to Ashley and Aadil.

Inside, each found a one-hundred-thousand-dollar check with their names neatly typed.

"Consider it a small token of appreciation," the General added. "Have fun, recharge, and come back ready."

They both thanked him and left the building smiling, the tension of months in Pakistan finally lifting.

Aadil opened a new bank account and deposited his check immediately. Ashley placed hers into her existing account. She had always been careful with money, preferring to save rather than spend.

The next morning, Ashley walked into the District Court building for the first time in almost a year. The familiar scent of old paper and polished wood instantly grounded her.

Her colleagues were shocked and thrilled to see her.

"Ashley? You're back?" her senior attorney, Martha Greene, exclaimed, rushing to hug her. "We thought you disappeared for good."

Ashley laughed. "Not yet. I have about four or five months free and thought I'd help with the caseload, if you'll have me."

Martha exchanged a glance with Lisa, the firm's fast-talking paralegal.

"Have you?" she said. "We're drowning in cases. We could use every good lawyer we can get."

Lisa quickly pulled up her schedule. "Let's set up a meeting tomorrow morning. We'll get you caught up and back on the docket."

Ashley nodded. "Perfect."

As she left the courthouse, she felt something she hadn't felt in months, a sense of normalcy.

She looked up at the American flag fluttering above the courthouse steps and whispered to herself, "Back to justice, even if only for a little while."

Ashley's first week back at the District Court came with a physical abuse and harassment complaint against a police officer, filed by a young Black nurse.

Ashley stayed in her office late, reading the file under the glow of her desk lamp.

The nurse, driving home after her hospital shift, was pulled over at eleven thirty p.m. The officer claimed to be conducting an alcohol test. Exhausted and still in her scrubs, she explained she'd been on a long shift from three to eleven. The officer ignored her, handcuffed her roughly, and accused her of resisting arrest. Only after another patrol car arrived and confirmed her identification and hospital badge did they release her.

Ashley shook her head. "Humiliating and unlawful," she muttered.

She called out to her law clerk. "Lisa, do we have the police car's dashcam footage?"

"Not yet," Lisa replied. "We'll have to request it through the court."

Ashley nodded. "Do it first thing tomorrow."

A week later, the client walked into Ashley's office, young, professional, and visibly nervous. Ashley greeted her with warmth and professionalism.

"Thank you for coming in," Ashley said. "Let's go over everything in your own words."

Ashley recorded the complete statement, then began her standard interview.

"How often do you drink?"

"Hardly ever. My father was an alcoholic. He abused my mother. I hate alcohol."

"Any history of drug use or DUIs?"

"Never. My last traffic ticket was five years ago."

"And you've been a nurse for five years?"

"Yes, ma'am."

Ashley smiled. "Good. I believe you have a strong case. Now, where exactly did this happen?"

"At the junction of Kingsway and Hampton Avenue."

Ashley wrote it down carefully. "Perfect. We'll contact you once the court date is set."

The next afternoon, Ashley drove to the intersection. She noticed traffic light cameras mounted on the signal poles. Bingo.

Back at the office, she turned to Lisa again.

"Do you still know anyone at the city's traffic video department?"

"Maybe. There used to be a girl named Amanda, but I'm not sure if she's still there."

Ashley smiled. "Let's find out."

That evening, she went to the City Traffic Control Center. Amanda's shift hadn't started yet, but a helpful technician at the front desk greeted her.

"Can I help you, ma'am?"

"Ashley Smith, Public Defender's Office. I need footage from the Kingsway and Hampton junction, specific date and time."

The man nodded, recognizing the urgency in her tone. Within minutes, he pulled up the footage. Ashley leaned in as the screen played the entire stop. Everything her client had said checked out perfectly, the officer's aggression, the lack of any reason for the arrest, and the nurse's calm demeanor.

"Can I get a copy of that recording?" Ashley asked.

"Normally, I'd need supervisor approval," he said, "but since you're Amanda's friend, I'll make an exception. Got a memory stick?"

Ashley smiled and handed one over. "You're a lifesaver."

"Buy me dinner sometime instead," he grinned.

She laughed, then remembered she had a restaurant gift card in her car. She returned moments later and handed it to him.

Later that night, Ashley showed the video to Lisa.

Lisa gasped. "This is gold. You just won the case before it even started. We don't even need a subpoena for the police recording."

Ashley nodded, satisfied. "Let's file it."

She prepared a lawsuit against the officer and the city police department for physical abuse, harassment, and discrimination.

Within two months, the court issued a subpoena and set a hearing date.

The courtroom was tense. The prosecutor, a seasoned but arrogant district attorney, barely looked at his notes. The officer, sitting beside him, wore the same defiant smirk seen in the video.

The district attorney stood first.

"Your honor, my client maintains that the suspect was driving recklessly, possibly under the influence, and became combative when officers attempted to administer a sobriety test."

Ashley rose calmly.

"Your honor, every word my colleague just said is false. Rather than a speech, I'll let the truth speak for itself."

She handed the flash drive to the clerk. The judge watched the footage in silence until the room grew heavy with embarrassment.

Finally, the judge looked up, visibly angry.

"Counselor, your client's behavior is unacceptable. Ms. Smith, your evidence is clear and decisive."

Ashley nodded slightly. "We seek fifty thousand dollars in compensation and a formal written apology to my client."

The gavel hit the bench.

"Granted. The City Police Department will issue a written apology and pay full compensation."

The nurse burst into tears, hugging Ashley. "Thank you. You gave me my dignity back."

Back at the firm, Martha smiled proudly. "That's incredible."

Ashley shrugged modestly. "Sometimes, it's not about fighting harder. It's about preparing better."

That evening, over dinner, Aadil congratulated her.

"You're amazing. Another win, easy for you."

Ashley smiled. "Thanks. But honestly, many senior attorneys don't prepare their cases. The worst are lazy government prosecutors. They win because the system helps them, not because they're right."

She sighed. "Most judges lean toward the government. Justice shouldn't depend on favoritism."

Still, she smiled. One case closed, and maybe one more before the holidays, if the docket didn't freeze for December and January.

Lisa promised to update her if any new cases came up.

For now, Ashley finally fell back into her element, calm, sharp, and exactly where she belonged.

CHAPTER 19: PENTAGON – MISSION BRIEFING, MID-MARCH

Time, as always, has its own pace. It rushes when life is good and crawls endlessly when times are rough.

For Aadil and Ashley, the five months in America passed in a blur of calm days, warm family dinners, and quiet nights free of fear. But as the end of March approached, it was time to prepare again.

They began packing carefully: laptops, encrypted phones, and all the gear they would need once more in Pakistan. Two weeks before departure, they were called to the Pentagon for a mission briefing.

Inside a secure conference chamber, the new mission team waited. The walls were lined with satellite maps of northern Pakistan. The rugged terrain of NWFP, Gilgit, and the upper tribal belt glowed under red digital grids.

At the head of the table stood General Mark Milley, who now oversaw the operation.

"Welcome back, both of you," General Milley said. "Your work last year was exceptional. The devices you placed have been fully functional. We've been intercepting transmissions between ISI field units, local tribal leaders, and several Taliban commanders."

He paused, pressing a button that zoomed the digital map closer to the Afghan border.

"However," he continued, "there's still no direct signal or trace of Bin Laden. That's where this year's mission comes in."

Ashley and Aadil leaned forward, studying the map.

"This year, your objective is more challenging," General Milley said. "You'll be deploying the new high-frequency, long-range satellite interceptors, the next generation of what you used last year. They're lighter, more durable, and capable of picking up micro-bursts of encrypted communication from over fifty miles away. But to maximize signal coverage, these devices must be placed at the highest possible elevations. The more altitude, the clearer the intercept."

Ashley frowned slightly. "High mountains? As in actual climbing?"

General Milley smiled. "Yes, Ms. Smith. We'll need your partner's experience there."

He turned to Aadil. "You used to climb and hike in those regions, correct?"

"Yes, sir," Aadil said. "I know the terrain well. The Karakoram and Hindukush ranges aren't easy, but I've trained there before."

"Good," General Milley said. "That's why we want you to lead the field placements. Dr. Afridi will handle coordination and data monitoring from the Islamabad base. He's excellent at analysis, but he's not built for mountain air."

The room laughed softly.

"As usual," General Milley continued, "you'll start your UNO polio vaccination campaign first. That gives cover for your movement and re-establishes your presence in the region. You'll be working the same way: public health on the surface, signal intelligence beneath it."

He glanced down at the materials in front of him.

"As you've seen in the technical briefing, these new-generation tracking devices are far superior to anything previously deployed in the field. Each unit can intercept and record any wireless signal within a fifty-mile radius, whether it's military communication, a walkie-talkie channel, or a civilian phone call. They'll capture everything that crosses their frequency band."

He continued without looking up. "This technology isn't even on record. They sync directly to the Navy's satellite command network stationed in the North Arabian Sea. Once deployed, they'll relay through secure frequency bands invisible to local scanners."

He looked at both of them, his tone measured and deliberate.

"As before, you'll collect the full set of devices from Dr. Afridi once you're settled in Islamabad. Your operational cover remains the same, the UNO polio vaccination campaign, but your primary task will be to place only twenty to thirty of these units in the highest possible locations. The mountains will give you range and protection. You'll have to hike, climb, and choose sites that are remote, hidden, and unlikely to be disturbed."

He looked toward Aadil. "You know the terrain. I trust your judgment on which peaks and ridges can be accessed safely."

Then he turned to Ashley. "You'll maintain the logs and coordinate each placement through Afridi's encrypted channel. No rush. Two or three devices per week is ideal. This isn't about speed. It's about precision and stealth."

Ashley nodded. "Understood, sir. We'll pace the operation and keep it clean."

Aadil added, "We'll make sure every placement counts."

"Good," General Milley said. "The fewer trips, the better. You'll be out there alone most of the time. Stay alert, avoid patterns, and remember, the mountains keep their own secrets."

They both nodded, fully aware that this second phase would be riskier than the first, and possibly the most critical step toward finding Bin Laden.

"Now, about security," General Milley said. "ISI surveillance has intensified since last winter. They know someone's been operating in those northern sectors. You'll need to rotate travel patterns, use secondary routes, and limit radio use. Trust no one outside the UNO chain."

Ashley nodded, quietly determined. "Understood, sir."

"We'll adapt," Aadil said. "And this time, we'll go higher and deeper."

General Milley smiled. "That's what I want to hear. You two are the perfect balance: Afridi for the desk, Aadil for the mountains, and Ashley for the diplomacy. That's why this mission works."

He handed them sealed envelopes.

"These contain your travel clearances and local ID renewals," he said. "You'll depart in ten days."

He paused one last time.

"This might be the year we finally get the breakthrough we've been waiting for. Stay sharp. Pakistan in the spring looks peaceful, but you know better."

Ashley and Aadil exchanged a look, half excitement, half apprehension.

They landed at Islamabad International Airport early Thursday morning, where the UNO driver was already waiting to pick them up. The drive to Haripur felt familiar now: the winding roads, the distant peaks, and the blend of spring dust and mountain air.

When they reached their villa, Aadil did a quiet inspection of every room. Nothing was out of place. He had deliberately left a few small markers, a book slightly tilted, a paper folded under the lamp, to test whether anyone, especially ISI, had entered while they were gone. Everything was exactly as they'd left it.

The next day, Friday, Aadil's mother and Yasser's family came to visit. The house was filled with laughter and the smell of home-cooked food. His mother couldn't hide her happiness seeing both Aadil and Ashley again after months.

By Monday, they reported back to the local UNO office in Haripur. Their old team welcomed them warmly. Aadil led the first staff meeting.

"Our first goal," he said, "is to identify all the children born in the last five months. We need to reach their parents quickly and convince them about the importance of polio vaccination. Please contact every local midwife. They're our best connection to new families."

Both Lady Health Visitors nodded. They already had lists of new births and good relations with most of the village midwives.

Ashley added with enthusiasm, "This year, we'll invite all the midwives to our office. We'll give each of them one hundred dollars to attend the session. It's not just payment. It's appreciation."

The LHVs exchanged surprised smiles. In those rural areas, a hundred dollars was generous money, enough to feed a family for weeks.

Aadil supported her idea immediately. "Yes, it's a good incentive. They'll help us spread awareness faster. We'll share our field allowance with them if needed."

Ashley then turned to the two vaccination teams. "We'll also add a performance incentive this year. The team that vaccinates the most children will receive a two-thousand-dollar reward at the end of the campaign."

The staff cheered. Motivation spread through the room.

Over the next two months, Aadil and Ashley threw themselves into the work. They revisited every Basic Health Unit, Rural Health Center, tehsil, and district hospital, and private clinic they had known from the year before. This time, their reputation preceded them. Doctors, nurses, and midwives greeted them with trust and familiarity.

CHAPTER 20:
CALL FROM DR. AFRIDI

After two months of intense fieldwork, Aadil and Ashley's UNO polio vaccination campaign was running smoothly. The local health teams were now confident and independent, and the villagers trusted them completely. The UNO van had become a familiar sight across Haripur and the northern valleys, a symbol of health, not suspicion.

One Friday morning, Ashley received a brief encrypted message on her secure UNO laptop: "Report to Islamabad headquarters. Saturday. 10:00 AM."

She showed it to Aadil without saying a word. They both knew it was from Dr. Afridi.

The next day, they drove quietly to Islamabad in the UNO bulletproof van. The moment they entered the building, they noticed small but unmistakable changes: tighter security, more surveillance cameras, and new faces at the reception. Dr. Afridi met them in the lobby and guided them straight to the restricted basement section, the same hidden level behind the large painting.

Inside, the operations room looked completely upgraded, with new monitors, updated computers, and rows of sealed metallic cases.

Dr. Afridi greeted them warmly. "Welcome back, my friends. You've done excellent work again. The CIA and Pentagon are very pleased with both of you."

He opened one of the metallic cases, revealing sleek, compact devices, far smaller than last year's models.

"These are the next-generation signal interceptors," he explained. "They can capture radio, satellite, and mobile transmissions within a 50-mile radius, even across mountain ridges. Each device is equipped with auto-encryption and long-life batteries. These can last up to ten years without maintenance."

Ashley leaned closer, inspecting one. "They're so small, like a cigarette box."

Dr. Afridi nodded. "Yes, that's the idea. Lightweight, waterproof, and heat-resistant. You can hide them in stone walls, under bridges, or even inside old vehicles. Once activated, they'll automatically connect to the U.S. Navy's satellite office in the North Arabian Sea."

He pulled up a large digital map on the wall, northern Pakistan and the Afghanistan border glowing with hundreds of signal dots.

"As per General Milley's new strategy, your task this year is precision, not quantity," he said. "We want 20 to 30 interceptors placed at high-altitude positions. The higher the elevation, the stronger the range. Especially focus near the Dir, Swat, and Kohistan regions. We believe there's renewed Taliban activity, possibly linked to Bin Laden's network."

Aadil studied the map carefully. "The mountains there are tough, steep, and isolated. But with the right timing, we can manage it."

"Exactly," said Dr. Afridi. "You'll go for mountain hikes on weekends. Two to three places per week are enough. No hurry, but maximum precision. Remember, winter is still months away. You have the summer and early fall to work."

Ashley asked, "Do we keep reporting through the same laptop encryption?"

"Yes," Afridi replied. "Use the same channel, but you'll receive a new digital code every ten days. I've also upgraded your laptops and phones. All communications will now route through a triple-layer encryption relay to avoid ISI or Chinese signal tracing."

He handed each of them a new, sealed bag containing devices, an upgraded satellite phone, and a small envelope of cash for emergencies.

"No contact with me unless it's critical," he added. "The ISI has tightened surveillance after last year's activity. I've also arranged a backup safehouse in case of emergency. Details are inside this sealed packet. Do not open unless necessary."

Aadil and Ashley nodded. They understood the risk.

Before they left, Afridi paused and looked at Aadil seriously. "You've both done more than anyone expected. But this mission is different. Someone in ISI suspects foreign interference in KPK. Be careful. If they start tailing you again, vanish immediately."

As they drove back to Haripur that evening, neither spoke much. The weight of the new mission, the danger, the secrecy, the growing suspicion around them, hung heavily in the air.

Ashley finally broke the silence. "This feels different this time."

Aadil kept his eyes on the road. "Yes. The deeper we go, the closer we get, and the more dangerous it becomes."

The UNO van sat parked outside the office while Aadil spread out a fresh topographic map on the table, red pins and a felt-tip pen at the ready.

"General Milley wants peaks," Aadil said. "He's thinking altitude = range. That's true on paper. But the mountains the Pentagon imagines are not where the movement happens."

He traced a finger along the border valleys, the old smuggling tracks, the river cuts.

"High ridges are controlled, army posts, observation towers, even drone lanes," Aadil continued. "They're obvious. You don't hide something where the army sleeps. Taliban and the old networks avoid the obvious. They move on lower terrain: river crossings, cave mouths, shepherd trails, abandoned mineshafts, ruined hamlets. They use tunnels and folds of the hills. That's where voices leak."

Ashley leaned in, absorbing every line. "So, we place for coverage of movement, not just raw range."

"Exactly," Aadil said. "A fifty-mile nominal radius from a summit looks good on a satellite, but if the summit is watched, the device dies the moment someone finds it. A device by a river ford or inside a tumbled wall near a village will hear more real chatter. It's safer and smarter."

He pointed to several lesser-known trekking spots, old tourist trails, disused shepherd stairways, and ridgelines that sit below army observation posts but overlook valley routes.

"We'll avoid main summits and army approaches," Aadil said. "We'll pick uncommon tourist tracks and forget passes. You can hike them; they're manageable and less patrolled. We can still get good elevation for range but stay under the army's radar."

Ashley smiled. "Three days for vaccination, then weekend hikes. Two devices each Saturday and Sunday. Slow, precise, no shortcuts."

They were back in Haripur for a weekend with nothing urgent on the schedule. The mountain air felt kinder now that the devices were in place and the vaccination rounds were running smoothly.

Ashley folded her hands around a cup of tea. "What do you want to do with the money this time?" she asked.

Aadil smiled. "I've been thinking, buy a house in the suburbs of Islamabad. Something under our names. A safe place for the family when we're in Pakistan."

Ashley's eyes lit up. "Even better, buy the land now and build next year. That way, we design it our way, and it's ready when we return."

"Perfect," Aadil agreed. "Yasser can keep the village house. I paid for it, but it's his home. He deserves it."

They spent the afternoon visiting new suburban developments outside Islamabad. Aadil's mother rode in the backseat, delighted with the latest Toyota Corolla.

They chose a 500-square-meter plot (one Kanal) in a quiet subdivision not far from Yasser's village, close enough for weekend visits, far enough for privacy. Ashley sketched out ideas on a hotel notepad: a small garden courtyard, a sunroom for Lucy, and a modest study where she could read case files when back home.

"We'll meet the builder next weekend," Ashley said, tucking the notepad into her purse. "I'll pick a basic plan, and we'll adapt it later."

Aadil reached over and squeezed her hand. "It feels good to plant something permanent for once."

They drove home as the sun fell behind the hills, two people who split their lives between relief work, secrets, and the quiet hope of a family home waiting in Islamabad.

At the end of the year, the UNO office buzzed with celebration. The vaccination records were the best they'd ever been, the highest coverage rate in the region since the program began.

The secret to success wasn't complicated. Aadil's $100 appreciation strategy for midwives had worked perfectly. Those small payments, a token of respect, had motivated them to reach every home, every newborn, every reluctant family.

The training sessions Ashley organized had also transformed the local teams. The midwives, once shy and uncertain, now spoke confidently to parents, explaining how the polio drops could save a child's future.

When the performance results were announced, the entire office clapped and cheered. The top vaccination team received their $2,000 bonus and proudly posed for pictures with Aadil and Ashley.

"This year," said the local UNO director, "we made real history. We reached more children than ever before, and saved more futures than we can count."

For Aadil and Ashley, it was deeply satisfying. Beyond their hidden mission and secret devices, this was the work that gave their cover meaning and reminded them why they'd started it all in the first place.

The year ended on a high note: successful fieldwork, motivated teams, and real progress against polio.

The year passed faster than either of them expected. By autumn's end, the mountain air grew sharp again, signaling the closure of another mission. Their final debriefs with Dr. Afridi at the UNO office felt almost routine now: a handshake, a quiet nod, and brief congratulations.

"Same procedure next year," he said, sliding a folder across the table. "But nothing new this time. Enjoy your winter break."

Ashley had already been in touch with her old law office for weeks, and by the time they landed in the U.S., a few minor cases were waiting for her. Nothing high profile, but as she said, "Something is better than nothing. Experience always counts."

Lucy, Ashley's mother, greeted them at the airport, beaming, holding a sign that read, "Welcome Home, My Heroes!"

She hugged them both so tight that Aadil nearly dropped his carry-on.

Back in their suburban house, life felt easy again. Ashley's firm didn't have any full cases for her immediately, but she assisted on a November trial. "A supporting role," she joked. "Like the backup attorney who saves the day quietly."

Meanwhile, Aadil reported to the Pentagon with their mission summary. Nothing major to report: the new tracking devices were placed across northern Pakistan's hills and peaks, all still active and transmitting. But there was frustration in Washington, still no verified signal or trace of Bin Laden.

General Milley frowned at the data feed. "We've spent years, millions of dollars, and still nothing."

Aadil leaned forward. "Sir, he's likely still in Afghanistan. Those mountains are honeycombed with tunnels, built during the Russian war. Unless we plant the next round of devices deep in Tora Bora, we'll keep missing him."

The general studied him for a long moment. "That's bold, Aadil. And dangerous. The Taliban still controls most of that territory."

Aadil only nodded. "Let me think about it. I'll give you a plan in March."

Before they left, the Pentagon clerk handed each of them a sealed envelope. Inside was a $100,000 check and a short note:

Thank you for your continued service. Enjoy your winter leave.

Back in the States, life slowed to a gentle rhythm. Ashley dove into case prep; Aadil took over the household with Lucy. Together, they made an unlikely kitchen team, Lucy teaching him recipes, Aadil mastering them all.

By December, he was cooking like a pro: roasted salmon, casseroles, and fresh bread. Every night, the house smelled of butter and garlic.

Ashley laughed when she came home one evening to find both wearing matching aprons. "You two have turned into a culinary army," she teased.

"Orders from headquarters," Lucy said with a wink. "Ashley doesn't lift a finger until her trial's done."

CHAPTER 21:
HEALTHCARE FRAUD TRIAL

Ashley recently concluded her involvement in a healthcare fraud trial that, unfortunately, resulted in a loss. Although it was not her own case, she served as an assistant to the lead defense attorney, Martha, providing extensive research, documentation, and courtroom support throughout the proceedings. Despite her diligence and preparation, prevailing in cases against the government remains an immense challenge within the federal judicial system.

In many federal district courts, government prosecutors tend to have a distinct procedural advantage, as judges often give greater weight to the prosecution's motions and objections. This imbalance can make it difficult for defense teams to present their arguments or evidence fully before the jury.

Ashley and her team observed that the jury's exposure to the full context of the defense case was limited, as many defense questions or exhibits were restricted or objected to by the prosecution and frequently sustained by the judge. As a result, the defense's ability to communicate key facts and counterarguments to the jury was constrained.

Moreover, systemic and social challenges remain evident in the justice system. Cases involving minority defendants, particularly Black, Asian, or Hispanic clients, often face additional implicit biases, which can influence courtroom dynamics and perceptions even before the trial begins.

Despite these obstacles, Ashley demonstrated strong professional commitment, assisting Attorney Martha in preparing a comprehensive defense and ensuring procedural integrity throughout the trial. Martha has since expressed sincere appreciation for Ashley's hard work, professionalism, and perseverance under pressure.

The legal team is now preparing for the appeal process, which will proceed following the sentencing date scheduled for March. They remain determined to pursue all available legal remedies and to continue advocating for fairness, transparency, and justice in the appellate phase.

Dr. Afridi closed the laptop lid and stayed sitting for a long moment, watching the rain streak through the window of his Islamabad office. Outside, the city moved on in its ordinary frenetic way, vendors calling, a mosque somewhere delivering the five o'clock call, but inside the hidden room, the air felt brittle, like glass about to crack.

He tapped the secure line, and the CIA director's face filled the monitor. No small talk. Just the hard blue light of late-night intelligence and the kind of tired courtesy people use when they must speak of bad news.

"Tell me," the director said.

Dr. Afridi drew in a breath. "They've been sniffing around the Haripur corridor," he said low and deliberately. "Last week, ISI vans were seen near the northern ridges. Yesterday, someone came into the UNO field office and claimed to be from the provincial health directorate. He asked questions about our foreign staff, about schedules, and who travels where. He didn't identify himself as ISI, but he didn't need to. He didn't search the place. He didn't have to. He left with more than he came with: a pattern of quiet pressure."

At the other end of the line, the director's expression didn't change, but Dr. Afridi could feel the calculus behind it shifting. "Did they find anything?" the director asked.

"Not physically. Not yet." Afridi's fingers traced the rim of his teacup. "But they're active. I've had reports: arrests in Waziristan, sweeps around Quetta. When they get a whiff of something, they round up anyone who looks suspicious: shepherds, truckers, even merchants who trade at the border markets. People disappear for days, sometimes weeks. The provinces are nervous. Baluchistan and the NWFP corridor have long lists of missing men. This is how they tighten a net."

There was a pause on the screen, long enough for the sound of a distant generator to fill the silence. "What do you recommend?" the director asked finally.

"Hold the Haripur team," Dr. Afridi said. The words felt like dropping a weight onto the table. "Delay their return. Don't let Aadil and Ashley come back to Islamabad, not until we know what the ISI is doing and how wide their sweep is. They're on winter leave in America now. Keep them there. We spin this to UNO as a routine operational pause: budgetary audit, seasonal suspension, anything to keep it plausible. I'll map safe routes and monitor SIGINT. If the ISI narrows the triangulation, we'll act fast. But we cannot risk them walking back into a net that's being tightened."

The director nodded once. "Send them the notice. Keep all channels encrypted. We'll stand by for your route plan."

The room smelled of coffee and recycled air. A polished oval table sat under a bank of screens showing a dozen satellite feeds, red dots pulsing over jagged mountain ranges. General Milley stood at the head, his face the same measured stone the press saw on television, but tonight his voice carried a different gravity.

"Aadil. Ashley," he said without preamble. "Thank you for coming on short notice."

At the far end of the table, the CIA Director, dark-suited and quiet, watched the pair with an almost pitiful look. For two years, the operation had been a slow, expensive grind. The devices they'd placed had worked. Intercepts had led to strikes, convoys disrupted, and men captured. The numbers on the screen were not lies: thousands of targets struck, a grim tally of enemies removed. But the cost, Milley admitted, was in children and villages. Collateral damage, he called it, and the room heard the phrase and the weight of it settled in their chests.

"We didn't find our primary target," Milley said. "Not yet. But the devices, your work, gave us a decisive advantage in a hundred engagements." He turned to the map. "Now the ISI is closing in on Haripur. Dr. Afridi recommends suspending the UNO mission. We need new tools and ideas. We need options."

Silence followed, the quiet that fills a moment when lives are being recalculated.

Aadil's hand rested on the back of his chair. He'd expected this, the pivot, the new risk. He spoke calmly, in that flat voice people learned to trust. "General," he said, "I have an idea. It's dangerous, but it's plausible." He looked at Ashley; her jaw tightened, but she kept still.

"What are you thinking?" the Director asked.

Aadil described a disguise that was practical, not theatrical, a life in motion rather than a false biography. He spoke of traveling the border routes as a merchant, of blending into trade, of moving goods, and sitting in tea stalls where men talked loudly and carelessly. He did not elaborate on mechanics. He sketched motives and risks. "I'll go where the roads go," he said. "I'll listen. If they talk, we'll hear them."

General Milley listened, then nodded slowly. "It's high risk. You'll be beyond immediate reach. The ISI presence in the borderlands is strong; any misstep could be fatal." He paused, then met Aadil's eyes. "If you do this, you go with full support. We'll provide cover and logistics, and Dr. Afridi will coordinate from Islamabad. But you accept the danger, and the limits of what we can do for you there."

Ashley's face had gone pale. She had imagined the mission would harden, but not like this, not him alone in the borderlands, not the long stretches of desert and checkpoints and quiet men who watch too closely. "You can't go alone," she said softly. "You're not just risking yourself. You're risking everything."

Aadil reached for her hand across the table. "You're staying here," he said. "You'll keep working the legal side, keep our ties in D.C. That's how this works. I'll send reports. I'll come back."

Dr. Afridi, who had listened from the shadows, stepped forward. He did not promise miracles. He promised cover, the kind that could be made with bureaucracy and influence, the quiet paperwork that made people look the other way. "We will give you what you need to move under civilian cover," he said, careful as always to keep the language non-actionable. "Nothing reckless. I will manage every detail from here."

General Milley's approval was clinical and final. "We'll authorize the mission," he said. "But remember this: every choice will be weighed against a human cost. You both know what you're asking for."

Ashley sat back. She tasted metal at the back of her mouth, the cold calculus of government work. She had fought in courtrooms for justice, argued for mercy, and for the small human truths that the state's machinery often swallowed. Now she watched the machinery deciding a man's fate on a different scale.

When they left the Pentagon, the air felt thinner, as if the capital had exhaled something they could not take back. Aadil and Ashley walked out together but separately, partners linked by a plan, each carrying a different kind of burden. She would go back to her files and her clients; he would step into a life of roads and small trades, listening for a man who had turned the world into a war.

That night, as the briefing dissolved into midnight traffic, Ashley pressed her face into Aadil's shoulder and whispered what she could not say aloud: "Come back."

He squeezed her hand and said nothing, because words now were small things against the machines and maps and decisions waiting for them at dawn.

The villa was quiet except for the small sounds of a house settling. Aadil sat on the edge of the bed, the low lamp casting long shadows. Ashley stood by the window, looking out at the courtyard where a single jasmine tree stirred in the night wind.

She didn't look happy. "You can't go alone," she said finally, her voice taut. "Not into Afghanistan, not like this."

Aadil reached for her hand. His voice was steady, but there was a tiredness in it that came from too many years of hard choices. "I'm sorry, Ashley. I know what you're thinking. I know what you're scared of."

He swallowed and kept going. "We must do something different. The Pentagon is frustrated. I don't blame them. This will be our third year on this. We've put devices in the hills, we've helped disrupt networks, but we didn't get our main target. I have one idea that might change the pattern. It's dangerous, but it's based on what I know: the roads, the markets, the way people move when there's no light."

Ashley turned, anger and fear braided together. "Your life belongs to the CIA? You say that like it's a fact to be shrugged off. You made a deal. That doesn't make it right."

Aadil closed his eyes for a second. "I chose this profession. I chose the trade-offs. I knew then, and I know now, there are limited choices: follow the orders and try to deliver results, or walk away and leave a lot of people in the dark. You know what they do to people who walk away. Do you remember the Mir Aimal Kansi story? He made a choice and paid for it. There are no tidy exits here."

Ashley flinched at the name, history with edges. She pressed her palm flat against the window glass as if she could hold the world in place. "So you go and risk everything. For what? More strikes? More villages?" Her voice broke. "I can't make sense of how we keep justifying the children who die."

Aadil's face softened. "Neither can I. None of us likes collateral. I don't sleep well because of it. But if we can find the network and the people who plan those attacks, we might reduce that harm in the long run. That's the hope I'm holding to. I promised you I'd come back. I promised your mother that I'd be careful. I meant both."

She looked at him, searching for an answer that would make the fear smaller. "You keep saying you'll be fine. You keep saying you'll come back. That's not a plan. That's a prayer."

He laughed once, without humor. "Prayers get answered sometimes. Plans are made at other times. I've thought this through. I won't go in blind. I'll have cover, support, and contingencies. Dr. Afridi is arranging what we need. General Robert knows. You'll be here holding the line, your clients, your practice, our home. We work in different theaters now. That's how it must be."

Ashley let out a slow breath. She pictured him on a hot road, markets and smugglers and men who never slept in the same place twice. She pictured the phone calls she'd taken at three in the morning. She pictured a casket she couldn't imagine.

"What about us?" she asked, not wanting the answer.

He tightened his grip on her hand. "What about us? Why do I do this? I don't want to let you or General Robert down. I won't let your trust go to waste. I'll be careful. I'll come back."

She walked to him and sat beside him on the bed. For a long minute, they said nothing. Words felt small in the space between them.

"You're not going to be perfect," Ashley said finally, the lawyer in her surfacing in the plainness of the sentence. "None of us is. But don't make the mistake of thinking silence is agreement. If this mission changes who you are, we must know before you leave."

Aadil closed his eyes and rubbed his thumb along her knuckles. "If anything changes, you get a call, you get a message, you use the contingency. You disappear. Promise me you'll protect what's ours here if I can't."

She bit her lip, then nodded. "I promise."

They sat in the thin lamplight, two people threading themselves to a future that could be kinder or crueler. Outside, the jasmine smelled softer than ever. Inside, they tightened the small promises that would have to be enough until the world made its next decision.

CHAPTER 22:
THE NEW IDENTITY

The rain had been falling all morning over Langley, steady, gray, and soft against the tinted glass of the CIA complex. Aadil sat in the waiting area, clean-shaven except for a new beard trimmed to a sharp Pashtun edge, his eyes hidden behind cheap aviator sunglasses. The name on the manila envelope resting on his lap wasn't Aadil Gul. It was Gul Khan, a truck driver.

When the secretary called his name, Aadil stood and followed her down the narrow corridor to a small, windowless office. The room smelled of paper, printer toner, and coffee that had been sitting too long. The woman behind the desk, efficient and unreadable, slid a form toward him.

"Your new documentation, Mr. Khan," she said, deliberately using the alias. "The Director's office will finalize your new passport within two weeks. You'll receive it through secured diplomatic mail, along with your cover story, route instructions, and contact details in Dubai."

Aadil nodded, calm but alert. "Understood." He handed her the envelope. Inside were the latest photo, fingerprints, and his signature, written in slightly uneven Urdu script. The image on the ID barely looked like him anymore: darker hair, heavier beard, tired eyes. He looked like a man who had driven too many roads under too many suns.

The secretary scanned the documents, verified the details, and then looked up at him. "Once you get the package, follow the travel order exactly. No personal contact with anyone outside our chain of communication. You're off-grid starting now."

Aadil exhaled slowly. "Yes, ma'am."

As he turned to leave, she added, "Good luck, Mr. Khan." The words were polite, but they carried weight, a quiet acknowledgment that this wasn't a mission; it was a crossing into shadow.

Outside, Aadil walked through the drizzle to the parking lot. He opened the car door and sat for a long moment, watching the windshield wipers slide back and forth. He thought of Ashley, probably in court, pacing before a judge, her mind sharp and full of fire. He thought of his mother, who still believed he worked for the United Nations, helping children walk again.

They didn't need to know the rest.

He started the engine, pulled out onto the wet Virginia road, and said softly to himself, "Gul Khan. Welcome to your new life."

Four weeks later, a sealed envelope arrived at Aadil and Ashley's quiet suburban home in Virginia. The label was plain, no sender, no insignia, but both knew where it had come from: Langley, Virginia.

Aadil slit open the heavy paper carefully. Inside were the tools of a new life:

• A Pakistani passport under the name Gul Khan, complete with Dubai visa stamps and travel history from Peshawar to Dubai.

• A photo ID of a weary, middle-aged truck driver, the beard thick, skin weathered, the eyes darker and older than his own.

• A one-way ticket from D.C. to Dubai.

• A check for one million dollars, signed and sealed by the CIA's financial operations branch, the same amount Aadil had quietly requested at the last meeting.

He looked at the check for a long moment, then handed it to Ashley.

"Deposit it tomorrow," he said softly. "If something happens to me, I want you to be safe. At least financially."

Ashley's hands trembled as she took it. "Don't say that," she whispered, her eyes glassy. "You'll come back. You always do."

Aadil smiled faintly, trying to hide his own fear. "Yes, and no," he said after a pause. "Yes, I'm nervous. Leaving you alone is the hardest part. But no, I'm not afraid of the mission. I've lived too many lives under too many names. This one is just another mask."

Ashley looked at him, searching for the man she loved behind the beard and forged identity. "You're not just another name, Aadil," she said, her voice breaking. "You're my husband. Please come back."

He took her face in his hands and kissed her forehead. "I promise, I'll do everything I can."

At Dulles International Airport, the air was heavy with the scent of coffee, fuel, and rain-soaked asphalt. Aadil wore a worn leather jacket, faded jeans, and scuffed shoes, the look of a man who had worked the docks, not the corridors of power. Ashley stood beside him, clutching his arm, her eyes fixed on the departure gate.

"They said Malik will meet me at the Dubai airport," Aadil said, checking his ticket. "Dr. Afridi trusts him. He'll get me the truck, the IDs, everything."

Ashley nodded silently. Words had run out hours ago. She just held his hand, unwilling to let go.

When the final boarding call echoed through the terminal, Aadil turned to her and smiled, the same warm smile that had once convinced her to follow him across continents and into the unknown.

"I'll be back in eight to ten months," he said. "Maybe sooner."

Ashley tried to answer, but her voice caught in her throat. Tears welled in her eyes. "Just come back, please."

Aadil hugged her tight, holding her longer than usual, as if memorizing the feel of her heartbeat. Then, without looking back, he walked toward the gate.

Ashley watched him disappear into the line of passengers boarding for Dubai.

Through the glass, she saw the plane taxi onto the runway, a silver bird vanishing into a gray sky.

She pressed her hand to the window and whispered, "Come back to me, Aadil."

They met in the shade of the arrivals canopy, heat already softening the glass towers into a mirage. Malik was shorter than Aadil had pictured, thick-shouldered, hair gelled back, an easy smile that didn't quite reach his eyes. He moved with the practiced calm of a man who'd shepherded strangers through tricky borders more than once.

"Gul Khan?" he said, checking the name on Aadil's ticket.

"Aye," Aadil answered, keeping the new alias in his mouth like something he was learning to pronounce.

Malik shook his hand and led him to a waiting car. The drive to the small hotel near the creek was quick: glittering skyscrapers gave way to older neighborhoods, the air smelling of cardamom and diesel. At the hotel, Malik produced the paperwork, neat, official-looking pages that bolstered the story written into the passport.

"You'll stay here a week," Malik said as he handed Aadil a simple room key. "Dubai is for the layover: paper, final checks, and wash your accent if you must."

He sat on the edge of the bed and handed over a plain plastic-wrapped phone. "This is a local number. Prepaid. Drivers in Peshawar use phones like this. It's already registered under your name. Use it only for work." The message was short and to the point. They would not be sloppy, not here.

Malik then laid the rest of the cover on the bed like props in a play: a laminated work-permit card for a Dubai logistics firm (with dates that covered the last five years), a faded tenancy document showing a residence in Peshawar, and a driver's license in Gul Khan's name. "Your residency in Dubai will expire next week," Malik said. "Contract finished. Without that UAE employment visa or UAE work permit, you cannot stay here. Now you're going home to drive your own truck. Plain story. Simple. Nobody questions a man who moves goods."

Aadil turned the documents over again. Each line was a small architecture of deceit, necessary, precise, cold. He felt that old, odd vertigo of a man standing on the seam between two lives.

Malik's tone softened for a second. "There will be a truck ready in Peshawar. A driver's rifle will be part of the normal kit for safety on those roads. Licensed weapon. No drama." He didn't elaborate; the unsaid held more meaning than any detail could. "You're expected to look like a man who has run the same route for years. Hands rough, clothes faded, manner reserved. Any questions?"

Aadil put the papers down. He thought of Ashley's face at the airport, the way she'd kissed his forehead. "No questions," he said, but his voice carried the weight of all the things he didn't ask aloud.

"Good. Get some rest," Malik said. "I'll pick you up at dinner. Tomorrow, we will visit the company and then a small office, not far from the port. That's ordinary paperwork. After that, the flight is arranged; you head to Peshawar with a crew that won't ask too many questions." He smiled again, a practiced merchant's smile. "Eat something later. You'll need strength for the roads."

Alone in the small hotel room, Aadil dressed the part without argument. He shaved slightly to the line the passport showed, widened his gait in the mirror until it felt believable. He put the phone into a hidden pocket and lay back on the bed, the ceiling fan turning lazily above him.

He thought of Ashley folding the check into her safe, of his mother keeping the house tidy and expecting a quiet winter. He thought of the village roads, of the markets where men exchanged gossip with their goods.

Outside, Dubai's skyline blinked. Inside, in the hotel's quiet, Gul Khan breathed for the first time. He told himself the trick: perform the life often enough, and it becomes less of a costume. He also knew the danger: adopting a new name didn't change the shape of the mountain ahead.

When Aadil arrived in Dubai after a long time, he was struck by the city's transformation, its towering skyscrapers, modern architecture, and vibrant tourism industry. The UAE has made remarkable progress in real estate and urban development, offering a lifestyle and amenities comparable to major global cities.

However, true and lasting progress lies in building strong foundations for infrastructure and innovation. While the UAE and several other Muslim-majority countries have achieved visible economic growth, many still rely heavily on Western nations for advanced technology, research, and industrial capabilities. To achieve sustainable development and self-reliance, these countries need to invest more in education, manufacturing, research, and technological innovation rather than depending solely on imported expertise.

At dusk, Malik texted: Dinner, seven. Don't be late.

Aadil closed his eyes and, for a single honest second, allowed himself to be exhausted. Then he dressed, buttoned his jacket, and went down to meet the man who would be the first keeper of his new story.

The logistics office smelled faintly of engine oil and printer ink. Rows of shipping manifests lay on the desk; men in hard hats moved between pallets with the easy economy of people who lived by timetables. Malik introduced Aadil and Gul Khan to a lean supervisor who gave a cursory nod and a list of routes. The handshake was brief and businesslike: the paperwork legitimized the story, and the story mattered more than the men who told it.

"Before you go," Malik said as they walked back toward the Creekside bazaar, "one last thing. You'll bring a small pack of gifts for your family: clothes, some sweets, maybe a cheap radio for the house. The more ordinary the present, the less anyone questions why a man leaves Dubai." He added with a grin, "Buy something for the kids. They always remember the one who brings toys."

Aadil laughed, and they began the quiet commerce of cover. Over the next five days, he moved through Dubai's markets like a man on a pilgrimage: stacked boxes of dates, a bright plastic toy train for a nephew, a bundle of warm scarves for his mother. He bought a simple tape recorder and a pocket camera, not because he needed them but because truck drivers carry small tools, little devices to record deliveries, receipts, or memories. The objects helped stitch a life together.

At dusk, he walked to the creek and called Ashley. Her voice was thin but steady; she asked about his shopping and laughed when he described bargaining over a toy truck.

"Get something for your mother," she said. "And one for me too, a little thing to remember you by."

"I will," he promised. Each promise felt heavier than the last.

The night before departure, Aadil put things in order. He ironed the shirts he would wear on the bus to Peshawar, checked the tiny camera's batteries, and tested the recorder's microphone.

Then there was the exchange that made the crossing feel irreversible. In the shadowed office where Malik kept keys and documents, Aadil placed his American passport and the small pile of personal items on the table.

"Keep them safe," he said.

Malik slid the passport into a locked drawer and tapped the wood twice. "You'll get them back when you return to the U.S.," he said. No sentiment, only business. "No travel on this passport. You travel on Gul Khan's papers now."

CHAPTER 23:
INTO THE DUST

The plane touched down at Peshawar International Airport, its tires screeching against the hot tarmac. Aadil didn't need to look out the window to know where he was. The heavy, humid air that seeped into the cabin carried the unmistakable scent of diesel, spice, and dust, a perfume that only this corner of the world could create.

Waiting outside the terminal was Karim, a quiet man with sharp eyes and the demeanor of someone used to watching without being seen. He lifted a small placard with the name Gul Khan scrawled across it.

"Welcome home," Karim said, offering a firm handshake.

Aadil smiled. "Feels like I never left."

They drove through Peshawar's narrow streets, motorbikes weaving between trucks, shopkeepers shouting in Pashto, and children darting through the alleys. The air shimmered with heat. Aadil sat in silence, scanning the city that had once been part of his past life.

Karim's house was small but clean. A sturdy pickup truck stood parked out front, dented, sun-faded, and perfect for a man like Gul Khan.

"This is your home," Karim said, handing him two sets of keys. "One for the house, one for the truck. I'll help you load everything tomorrow from the market. Your paperwork is ready: business permit, Afghanistan trade approval, and visa. You're officially a food supplier now."

Aadil nodded. Everything was in place. His identity, his truck, his story. He had walked deeper into the role so many times before that it almost felt natural.

That night, he stepped outside the small house and looked at the truck under the streetlight, its cargo bed empty, waiting for purpose. He could already visualize the sacks of rice, flour, lentils, sugar, and cooking oil piled high. He knew what hunger looked like; he had seen it in the eyes of the displaced. In Afghanistan, food was currency, trust, and disguise all at once.

By sunrise, the truck was loaded. Karim had helped him bargain with the wholesalers at the Khyber Bazaar, loading every inch of the pickup with essential goods.

"This should last a week," Karim said, brushing dust from his hands. "Your trade route is already approved. Just keep your papers ready if anyone asks questions."

Aadil laughed softly. "And if they ask too many questions?"

Karim met his eyes. "Then you become the simple truck driver again. The one who sells rice and dal, not secrets."

The first trip took him deep into Nangarhar province, the rocky roads winding like brown scars across the land. He moved slowly, making small stops in the villages along the way, drinking tea with shopkeepers, chatting with children, and handing out cheap sweets. He sold everything at half the market price. Soon, the word spread: Gul Khan, the generous trader from Pakistan.

Each stop gave him a chance to do what he was truly there for. When no one was watching, he'd slip behind a half-collapsed wall or an abandoned storage shed, quietly burying a small device no bigger than a deck of cards.

It wasn't rushed work. He moved deliberately, methodically, one location at a time, one week at a time. Every placement was marked by instinct and geography, valleys, ridgelines, and crossroads where voices carried far.

Sometimes he'd sleep in the truck, listening to the static of local radio stations and the distant echo of prayer calls. The nights were cold, the stars painfully close.

He was checked twice by Taliban patrols, tense moments that ended with simple inspections. They searched his truck for weapons, then waved him through after finding only food, salt, and kindness.

By the end of the first month, Aadil's face had become familiar. Villagers began to wait for him, women in shawls bringing jugs, children running behind the truck, old men nodding from porches.

He mapped his route like a soldier planning a campaign: one week each in the east, west, north, and south. In two months, he would cover the entire zone, every valley, every outpost, every hidden path. And if needed, he would come back a third month to make sure the net was complete.

The CIA wanted devices on mountaintops. Aadil knew better. He was putting them where the whispers traveled, in the villages, on the dirt roads, and beneath the world's notice.

By late September, Gul Khan had traversed nearly every road, valley, and village in the region. Six months of grueling travel, selling food to villagers, and secretly placing tracking devices had brought the operation to its planned conclusion.

He had visited some locations twice, leaving his contact number with trusted villagers, a simple gesture to ensure communication in the harsh, mountainous terrain. Those who lived higher up were already preparing for the long winter, storing all their supplies for months of snow and isolation. Gul Khan's deliveries were now woven into the rhythm of their survival.

Back at his modest residence in Peshawar, Aadil spread the large map across the table. He traced his route with a practiced hand, checking off villages, outposts, and hidden paths where the devices had been planted. Each mark represented a week of meticulous planning and careful movement, a silent web spanning a region where few outsiders dared to venture.

By the end of September, he had finalized his report and handed it over to Karim, Dr. Afridi's trusted assistant.

Karim studied it briefly, then smiled. "Dr. Afridi has read your report. He's delighted. He appreciated your work, and so did we. This has been a flawless operation, Aadil."

Aadil nodded quietly, the weight of the months of labor finally lifting. "Thank you," he said.

Karim continued, "Next week, you'll have your Dubai ticket. On paper, you'll return to work at the same logistics company as before for six months. Everything will look routine. In April, you'll come back here and repeat the same operation. Easy for you, but for most, this job would be impossible, too dangerous, too complex."

Aadil leaned back, allowing a small, satisfied smile to cross his face. He had done what few could: navigated mountains, negotiated with villagers, avoided Taliban patrols, and completed a mission that even seasoned operatives would consider suicidal.

"Multi-talented," Karim added. "That's why the ISI picked you first, and why Bin Laden himself trusted you. Not many could have done what you did."

Aadil's eyes flickered with quiet pride. "I just did what needed to be done," he said, voice calm but resolute.

Karim nodded, handing him the plane itinerary along with the UAE work permit. "Go get some rest. Dubai will be routine, just like they want it to appear. But here, you've changed the map. The network is in place. The work is done."

Aadil folded the report, placed it in the drawer, and looked out the window at the rugged terrain beyond Peshawar. This land had tested him, shaped him, and trusted him with secrets few would ever know.

He whispered, more to himself than anyone else, "Mission accomplished."

Ashley was relieved and overjoyed to see Aadil back safely in the United States. The months of worry, uncertainty, and endless phone calls finally lifted as she embraced him at the airport.

Within days, Aadil was scheduled to brief the Pentagon and CIA on the completion of his mission. Sitting in the conference room, maps spread across the table, he recounted every detail, the villages visited, devices planted, routes taken, and interactions with local villagers. Every step had been meticulously planned, every challenge navigated.

General Milley leaned forward, a solemn expression on his face. "Aadil, we understand it's frustrating that we haven't yet pinpointed Bin Laden's exact location. From the start, we knew this search could take a year or several. But we are proud of you. Your courage, commitment, and precision have not gone unnoticed. You delivered on every promise you made."

The CIA Director nodded in agreement. "Your work has given us unprecedented insight into communications and movements in the region. While the primary target remains at large, the intelligence network you've helped establish will guide our operations next year."

Aadil nodded, keeping his calm, professional demeanor. "Thank you, General. I will remain ready for the next phase, whenever it begins. I am glad the mission went as planned and that no complications arose during the operation."

This time, there was no envelope with cash or instructions. He had received it in advance before leaving, a precaution for Ashley in case anything happened to him. It was a small relief, a quiet reassurance that she and the family were financially safe.

After six long months apart, Aadil finally called home. His mother's voice trembled with joy at the other end of the line. Ashley had kept in touch with her throughout his absence, often offering vague reassurances about his "UNO work," while Yasser quietly maintained the cover story.

Yasser, ever dependable, updated Aadil about the progress of their new home near Islamabad.

"The construction's going great," he said proudly. "The Mediterranean design you both picked looks incredible, two stories, seven thousand square feet. It'll be ready next year."

Aadil smiled. He could almost see the cream-colored walls, the curved arches, and the terrace overlooking the hills. It was more than a house; it was a promise of peace after years of living between missions and secrets.

Then his mother's gentle voice came through, amused but insistent.

"Aadil, I'm happy you're home and safe. But both of you should start thinking about children," she teased.

Ashley, listening nearby, laughed. "Your mom and my mom must have the same script. Lucy's been saying the same thing for a year now."

Aadil chuckled. "I told her, we'll start a family when my missions are over, when I'm a free man again."

Ashley nodded, understanding but wistful.

Life in the U.S. settled into a comfortable rhythm.

Ashley immersed herself in her demanding job as a public defender. Her caseload had climbed to one hundred and thirty, mostly DUIs, domestic disputes, and child custody cases. "I'm learning every day," she told Aadil one evening. "Once I have a few more years of courtroom experience, I might join a private firm."

Aadil smiled warmly. "Or better yet, we'll start our own firm. You'll be the brilliant attorney, and I'll be your quiet partner in the background."

Ashley laughed. "We'll see, Mr. Dreamer. That's a little early for now."

While she spent her days in court, Aadil found peace in the kitchen with Lucy. He learned new dishes, mastered American-style breakfasts, and even experimented with fusing Middle Eastern and Western flavors. Every evening, the house smelled of home, garlic, fresh bread, and laughter.

Time moved fast that year, too fast. Between court filings, family dinners, and the quiet comfort of routine, the tension of his past missions felt like a distant shadow.

But both knew that shadow would return.

The world outside their peaceful home hadn't changed; only paused.

CHAPTER 25:
THE THREAD TIGHTENS

December in Washington carried the kind of cold that made people hurry into buildings and speak in shorter sentences. The Pentagon summoned them both on a gray morning. The conference room smelled of reheated coffee and paper. Ashley and Aadil sat across from General Milley and the CIA Director as a live intercept scrolled quietly on the screen, a rough, translated patch of static and voices lifted out of the mountains.

"I want you two here because this changes the conversation," Milley said without preamble. "We've intercepted a conversation between a Taliban commander and a senior cleric that references an 'Ameer.' They're explicitly talking about city life. They're not whispering from a cave; they're talking about the comforts of a life that looks ordinary."

The soundbite played again, fragmented, human, terrifying in its normalcy.

"...he prefers the city... he is protected... we move quietly," the translation read.

The room held its breath.

Aadil felt the old machinery in his head click into place. He'd lived on these borderlands and the innards of both countries long enough to see patterns where others saw only noise. He leaned forward.

"Wait," he said. "Think about where we've been looking. We've been hunting the edges: passes, ridgelines, caves. But the man who once sheltered SM and other high-level operatives wouldn't live where patrols and drones make patterns easy to see."

He spoke quietly; each sentence pulled from the instincts that had kept him alive for years.

"If he's alive, he's living where people assume he cannot be, inside the normal, inside the protected. The safest place is the place everyone thinks is safe: the shadows of power. High-ranking officers' neighborhoods, cantonment towns, or compounds with diplomatic or military cover. Somewhere within a fifty-mile radius of Islamabad. Not a cave, not a cave dweller, but someone with protection, a man who's been granted a kind of invisibility by being close to power."

The table went silent. The CIA Director's eyes met Milley's. Milley allowed himself the smallest, surprised smile.

"We've been looking at distance and altitude," he muttered. "Maybe we needed to look closer to home."

Ashley thought of the interceptions, the web of devices, the months of dusty roads her husband had driven.

"If that's true," she said, "we need to pivot carefully. This is political dynamite. Whoever hides someone like that inside the cordon of power will not react kindly." Her lawyer's brain immediately began calculating the civil and diplomatic fallout of any overt move. "We need indirect pressure and delicate monitoring, nothing that hands them a reason to crush the wrong neighborhood."

Milley nodded. "Exactly. We will not rush in. We'll increase urban SIGINT, human intel, and correlational analysis inside the fifty-mile ring. No overt raids. No public confrontations. Dr. Afridi, I want your best analysts to coordinate with our satellite feeds and HUMINT assets. Aadil, your field sense will be crucial in designing routes and plausible covers. Ashley, you'll remain stateside, but you'll be part of legal and diplomatic contingency planning. If we find him, this won't be a single strike. It will be an operation that must account for fallout."

Aadil felt a cold, steady resolve settle over him. For years, he'd thought the answer was wind, snow, and quiet places. Now the truth felt stranger: the hiding place might be inside the very system that claimed to oppose him. It was the sort of irony that could swallow a man whole.

Milley closed his tablet and looked up. "A new plan. Quiet and surgical. We shift the net inward, carefully. Thank you, Aadil. Your instincts are why you're here." He let that acknowledgment hang between them like a promise and a warning.

The fourth year of the mission began with a new layer of risk and resolve.

Aadil, now living and breathing under his forged identity, Gul Khan, made a strategic but straightforward request to the CIA and Pentagon: keep the same ID, same name, same cover story. Continuity meant credibility.

This time, his plan went beyond deliveries. He wanted to cultivate genuine relationships with Taliban commanders inside Afghanistan, to step into their circle, to earn their trust, to listen.

He also asked for a larger transport truck, arguing that his previous customers had placed bulk orders for rice, sugar, lentils, and oil. The smaller Toyota Hilux pickup would still be his tool for the mountain passes, narrow roads where only the fearless drove.

The Pentagon approved everything without hesitation. They would do anything to find Bin Laden.

What General Milley's secretary forgot to mention was that Aadil's absence had been noticed. His old customers in the remote Afghan villages had left dozens of messages on his dusty local phone. They were asking for their "brother Gul Khan" and his delivery truck to return soon.

Dr. Afridi's assistant, Karim, had already responded using Gul Khan's alias:

"Deliveries will start again in April."

He also added, quietly, to the CIA's encrypted report:

"Track the customers who buy in bulk. There might be a lead."

Aadil arrived in Dubai and met Malik at the airport, same protocol, same exchange. His U.S. passport vanished into a briefcase; his Pakistani one appeared in its place. Malik handed him an envelope containing his travel papers and a renewed UAE work permit, both stamped with the same logistics company's name.

"If anyone asks," Malik said, "you just finished six months of work in Dubai. Show your company ID and work permit. You're going home to Peshawar now."

Aadil nodded. He knew the script by heart.

When he landed in Peshawar, Karim was waiting, same white Corolla, same quiet greeting. "Salaam, Gul Khan. Welcome back."

They drove through the old bazaar and into the city's outskirts, where his truck and Hilux were already parked.

"Both are yours," Karim said. "Use the small one in the highlands. If anyone's watching, your routes will never be predictable."

Aadil smiled faintly. "They always are."

Within weeks, Gul Khan was back on the dirt roads, his truck heavy with food supplies: rice, wheat, sugar, lentils, cooking oil, all that the mountain villages lacked. He also carried something new: posters he had designed himself, printed with the faces of Mullah Omar and Bin Laden, smiling under the words "Our Heroes, Our Protectors."

He hadn't told anyone about this part of the plan, not even Dr. Afridi. It was his own idea. If he could appear loyal, he could move deeper.

Each poster carried a micro-tracking chip behind its backing.

One morning, as his pickup rattled along a mountain road, a group of Taliban fighters stopped him, dust, rifles, suspicion in every glance.

"You worked in Dubai?" one asked, flipping through his passport.

Aadil smiled, humbled. "Yes, for the logistics company, only winter work. The rest of the year, I bring supplies here for my brothers."

They nodded approvingly. Then one pointed at the stack of posters.

"What are these?"

"Messages," Aadil replied calmly. "To remind people not to fear the Americans, that our Ameers are still strong. Mullah Omar, Bin Laden, they are our pride."

The men's eyes softened.

"You are our brother now," the leader said, hugging him. "Come with us. Our camp is not far. You will eat with us tonight."

Aadil followed their jeeps deep into the mountains, to a hidden valley invisible even to the drones. His truck's CIA beacon silently pulsed on satellite screens thousands of miles away. Langley had strict orders: no drone strikes near that signal. Too many "friendly fires" had already burned the wrong faces, weddings, children, and informants.

That night, he broke bread with men who didn't know they were dining with a ghost from Langley. They talked about faith, the cold, and the border raids. Aadil listened, smiled, and memorized faces.

Before leaving, he asked their commander, a former provincial governor, for permission to place posters along the roads.

The man laughed warmly. "Alhamdulillah, yes. Place them wherever you wish. And come back alone. Fewer people mean more safety from the drones."

"Exactly," Aadil agreed. "One truck, one man, less risk for all of us."

"Marhaba, brother Gul Khan. You are one of us now."

The next morning, Aadil left the valley, placing the posters and the hidden tracking devices near the Taliban hideouts.

When he reached Peshawar, he sent a coded report:

"Posters placed. Targets active. Recommend a ceasefire for now."

He told the Pentagon and Dr. Afridi that the drones needed to stop, at least for a few months.

"Let them think the U.S. has stopped hunting," he said. "Once they relax, they'll move, and we'll see where."

The Pentagon agreed.

And within weeks, the radio chatter changed. Taliban groups spoke more freely. The CIA began intercepting fragments, new voices, coordinates, and references to "the Ameer."

Aadil's network of "deliveries" grew. Every few days, a new mountain road. Every third day, another remote village.

He was no longer just a supplier. He was trusted.

Within three months, he had quietly mapped the locations of half a dozen Taliban compounds and collected phone traffic that mentioned the name Bin Laden more times than in the last two years combined.

Langley called it "the Gul Khan Breakthrough."

Aadil called it progress with a price.

CHAPTER 26:
THE HIDDEN VALLEY MEETING

The mountain air was thin and carried a biting chill that seeped through the canvas of Aadil's truck. His third month driving supplies into the deepest, most forgotten folds of the Hindu Kush was supposed to be his last. This delivery, a special request of rice, flour, and canned goods, had taken him to a place where the very maps seemed to blur.

The compound was a cluster of mud-brick houses clinging to the mountainside, a place of shadows and whispers. As night fell, the commander, a man with a beard like a bird's nest and eyes of flint, offered him a place by the fire. It was then that Aadil noticed them.

They were out of place. Their features, their posture, the cut of their clothes beneath the local shalwar kameez, it all whispered a different origin. Indian, he thought. He kept his head down, playing the part of the simple, tired driver, but his senses, honed by a previous life, were screaming.

He pretended to doze by the dying embers of the fire, his ears straining. The visitors spoke in low tones with the Taliban commander. Their leader, a man with a hawk-like nose and a deceptively calm voice, was fluent in Pashto, but his accent betrayed him. Aadil, who had spent years listening in the shadows, understood every word.

"We share a common grief," the hawk-faced man was saying. "Pakistan occupies lands that are historically Afghan, Baluchistan, and the tribal areas. This is an injustice."

The commander grunted, his expression unreadable.

"We wish to help you correct this," the man continued, leaning forward. The firelight caught the sharp planes of his face. "India will provide you with money, weapons, and everything you need. Your task is simple. Train the local boys who come to you. Train them not just to fight, but to become thunderclaps. Send them back across the border as martyrs, in the name of Jehad. The ISI has spilled much Taliban blood. It is time for revenge."

Aadil's blood ran colder, colder than the mountain night. This wasn't just an insurgency; it was a meticulously planned poison.

The Indian leader gestured, and one of his men brought forward a heavy, metal-reinforced suitcase. The click of the latches was unnaturally loud in the silent night. He opened it. Neat, bound blocks of US dollars lay inside, a green sea of temptation. The Taliban commander's eyes, for the first time, flickered with avarice.

"This is merely a beginning," the hawk-faced man said, closing the case with a definitive thud. "We have the logistics, the inside information. Our network is already active in Quetta and in Waziristan. We will guide you to the most impactful targets." He paused, letting the offer hang in the air. "If you have questions, our group leader is Major Yadhav. He will be your point of contact."

Aadil remained motionless, but his mind was a storm. As an ex-ISI agent, he knew the region's dirty chessboard intimately. He knew of Indian spies probing the vulnerabilities of Baluchistan, just as he knew of ISI assets deep in Kashmir and Punjab. It was the unspoken war.

But this was different. The sheer audacity, the cold, transactional nature of it, the explicit goal of carving up his nation, to ultimately sever Baluchistan and see it join Afghanistan, was a blade to the gut. The theoretical knowledge of a shadow war was one thing; hearing its execution planned over a suitcase of cash in a remote mountain compound was another.

He stared into the dying fire, the ghost of the dollars imprinted on his vision. The simple driver was gone. The ex-agent was back, and he was the only one who carried a truth that could ignite a war or prevent one. The long road back to Pakistan had just become the most dangerous journey of his life.

Aadil felt his stomach knot. The plan was brutal and pragmatic: to turn local grievances into a proxy campaign. He knew at once what the implications would be, not just for the valley, but for the whole region. He pressed the details into memory: the group's name, the leader's cadence, the mention of a senior operative called Major Yadhav.

During a visit to western Baluchistan, Aadil observed several foreign companies involved in mineral extraction. Baluchistan is known to be exceptionally rich in natural resources, including copper, gold, iron ore, chromite, coal, marble, barite, and lead-zinc. Recent geological surveys also indicate the presence of rare-earth elements such as cerium, lanthanum, and neodymium, along with traces of thorium and uranium.

The well-known Reko Diq project in the Chagai District is one of the world's largest undeveloped copper-gold deposits. Other areas, such as Sendak, also contain significant mineral reserves. Despite this immense potential, economic instability and governance challenges have limited the benefits these resources offer to local communities and the national economy.

Analysts have noted that political instability, weak regulation, and corruption have made it difficult for Pakistan to realize the potential of its mineral wealth fully. As a result, the country continues to depend heavily on international financial assistance, including from the IMF.

He knew what he'd just witnessed could shift the entire mission.

He would have to get word to Dr. Afridi carefully. One wrong move, and the valley would become his grave.

Most Used Daily Food Items by Middle Eastern

Aadil studied in more detail the daily groceries consumed by most of the Arabic community. He would like to get an idea of where Bin Laden and his associates get those supplies.

The daily diet in Saudi Arabia, and much of the Middle East, is built on a foundation of flavorful, wholesome, and versatile ingredients.

Here is a list of the most used daily food items, categorized for clarity.

1. *Staples & Grains*

These are the absolute foundations of most meals.

- Rice: The king of Saudi cuisine. Long-grain basmati rice is the most common, often served as a bed for stews and grilled meats.
- Bread (Khubz): Eaten with almost every meal.
- Khubz Arabi: The ubiquitous, round, flat, white pita bread.
- Tamees: A slightly thicker, chewy bread, often baked in a tandoor oven. A breakfast staple.
- Samoli: Small, crusty baguette-like rolls.
- Wheat (Burghul): Cracked wheat, used in dishes like Tabbouleh and Kibbeh.
- Freekeh: Smoked green wheat has a nutty flavor and is often used in savory dishes as a rice alternative.

2. *Proteins*

- Chicken: The most widely consumed meat, prepared in countless ways (grilled, stewed, roasted, as shawarma).
- Lamb & Mutton: Favored for special occasions and traditional dishes like Kabsa and Mandi.
- Beef: Commonly used in stews and ground for dishes.
- Fish & Seafood: Especially common in the coastal regions (Eastern Province, Jeddah). Shrimp and hamour (a type of grouper) are popular.
- Lentils & Chickpeas: A vital and inexpensive source of protein, used in soups, stews (like Harees), and dips (Hummus).

3. *Dairy & Dairy Substitutes*

- Labneh: A thick, strained yogurt cheese, eaten for breakfast with olive oil and za'atar, or as a dip.
- Yogurt (Laban): Consumed plain, as a drink (Laban Ayran, a salted yogurt drink), or used in cooking.
- White Cheese (Jibneh Baida): A salty, brined cheese like feta or halloumi, but less rubbery. Eaten for breakfast.
- Milk (Laban): Used in drinks, desserts, and sometimes in Arabic coffee.

4. *Vegetables & Fruits*

- Tomatoes & Tomato Paste: The base for most stews and sauces.
- Onions & Garlic: The essential flavor base for virtually all savory cooking.
- Cucumbers & Tomatoes: The classic fresh salad combination, eaten daily.
- Eggplant (Aubergine): Used in dips (Baba Ghanoush), stews, and as a side dish.
- Potatoes: Often fried or included in stews.
- Okra: A key ingredient in popular stews like Bamiyah.

- Dates (Tamr): A cultural and religious staple. Eaten daily, especially to break the fast during Ramadan, and offered to guests as a sign of hospitality.
- Citrus Fruits: Lemons are used constantly, both fresh and as bottled juice, for dressing and flavoring.
- Melons, Grapes, & Pomegranates: Common and popular fruits, especially as desserts.

5. *Herbs, Spices & Flavorings*

This is where the iconic flavors come from.

- Parsley & Mint: Used abundantly in salads, garnishes, and meat dishes.
- Coriander (Cilantro): Frequently used in cooking.
- Black Pepper, Cumin, & Coriander Seeds: The holy trinity of spice blends.
- Cardamom (Hill): The signature spice of Arabic coffee and also used in many meat dishes and desserts.
- Saffron & Turmeric: Used to give rice a beautiful yellow color and distinct flavor (essential for Kabsa).
- Cinnamon & Cloves: Used in both sweet and savory dishes.
- Tahini: A paste made from sesame seeds, used in hummus and sauces.
- Pomegranate Molasses: A tangy, sweet-sour syrup used in dressings and glazes.
- Olive Oil (Zait): Drizzled on everything from hummus and labneh to salads.

6. *Common Daily Dishes Featuring These Items*
- Breakfast: Foul Medames (fava bean stew), Tamees bread, Labneh, white cheese, olives, and eggs.
- Lunch/Dinner:
- Kabsa: The national dish, spiced rice with chicken, lamb, or fish.
- Mandi: Similar to Kabsa, but the meat is slowly cooked in a tandoor, giving it a smoky flavor.

- Shawarma: Thinly sliced marinated chicken or beef rolled in bread.
- Saleeg: A white, creamy rice dish, usually served with chicken.
- Stews (Yakhneh/Maraq): Served with rice, featuring okra, eggplant, or potatoes with meat.

ENDING OF 4TH YEAR

For three straight months, Aadil had traversed nearly every corner of Afghanistan: deserts, high mountain passes, and remote valleys where maps turned blank. His next target zone lay across the border: the ring of towns and cities within fifty miles of Islamabad.

Before setting out, he met with Karim to discuss adding a new line of goods to his routes, specialty food items for Arab descendants who had settled across the NWFP, Baluchistan, and parts of Afghanistan. Aadil suggested importing dates, spices, and packaged Middle Eastern products that he could easily source through his "Dubai connections."

It was a clever move. Each new order, each casual conversation about familiar foods, gave him another reason to meet people who might otherwise stay hidden. Wherever he went, he mentioned, almost in passing, that he could get anything "straight from the Middle East" thanks to his winter work in Dubai.

By late September, the idea paid off. One evening, his phone rang. A voice on the other end spoke in accented Pashto, but with clear traces of Arabic. The caller asked discreet questions about his ability to import items from the Gulf. Aadil's instincts sharpened immediately. He explained that his job in Dubai gave him easy access to suppliers and that he would soon return there for the winter season.

"We will call again," the man said, before the line went dead.

Aadil sat for a moment, studying the silence. It was the first real sign. Someone close to the networks that protected Arab fighters in hiding might finally have reached out.

Weeks passed with no return call, but Aadil documented every detail. By the end of the month, he compiled his annual report and passed it to Karim. As per Dr. Afridi's standing instructions, there would be no direct meetings; ISI's surveillance had grown intense.

When his cover contract in Dubai officially ended, Aadil made the same familiar route: a flight from Peshawar to Dubai, then onward to Washington, D.C. Ashley was waiting at the airport, smiling as always when she saw him step through arrivals. For a moment, all the layers of deception and danger seemed far away.

CHAPTER 27: PENTAGON & CIA BRIEFING

The atmosphere in the secure briefing room was a complete reversal from their first, tense meeting. This time, the Pentagon team radiated a palpable, almost electric satisfaction. Where their postures had once been rigid and assessing, they were now relaxed, leaning forward with keen interest.

General Milley himself, a man whose face usually resembled a granite cliff, offered a rare, thin smile. "Aadil," he began, his voice low and deliberate. "That was more than just brave. It was brilliant. You've single-handedly provided a strategic clarity we've been missing for years." He paused, letting the weight of the praise settle in the silent room. "Your actions have confirmed your loyalty and your value to the United States, beyond any doubt."

The General's eyes locked onto Aadil's. "I'd like to continue our conversation privately. Just you and me. Next week, at my office?"

The exclusivity of the invitation hung in the air. "Yes, sir," Aadil replied, his voice steady. "I'll be there."

As they were dismissed, a secretary handed each of them a plain white envelope. Outside in the corridor, Aadil peeled his open. His breath caught. The check was made out for $1,000,000.00.

Ashley glanced at hers and let out a sharp, incredulous laugh. "Are you fucking kidding me?" She showed him the figure: a still generous, but vastly different, $100,000.00. "Holy crap, Aadil. A million dollars?"

"OMG," he whispered, staring at the life-changing number. "This is… a lot of money."

"It is," Ashley said, her joking tone vanishing, replaced by one of stark professional respect. "But the intel you pulled, what did you risk? It's worth ten times that. You saw them there. They're not just happy; they're excited. They got a major lead, something they're not sharing with us. My guess is that General Milley will be the one to tell you."

"I agree," Aadil said, folding the check and tucking it away as if it were a live grenade.

Ashley lowered her voice, stepping closer. "So, what's your reading? What does a one-on-one with Milley mean?"

"I have a theory," Aadil admitted, his gaze distant. "But I'd rather wait to hear it from him."

"Come on, Aadil. What do you think?"

He finally met her eyes, his expression grim. "They're going to ask me to keep an eye on the ISI and the Pakistani nuclear program."

Ashley's eyes widened. "Are you serious?"

"I could be wrong," he said with a shrug that didn't mask his certainty. "But it's the only guess that fits. For the CIA, for Mossad, for RAW, Pakistan's nuclear arsenal is the ultimate prize, and its biggest nightmare."

"Let's hope this is a good thing," Ashley said, though her voice was laced with concern. "This is a massive compliment, Aadil. The Pentagon and the CIA don't just hand out meetings and million-dollar checks. They're grooming you for a much bigger role in the region."

Aadil nodded slowly, the weight of the future pressing down on him. "Let's wait and see what the next meeting brings."

Secret Meeting with General Milley

The building was a fortress of concrete and silence, set apart from the rest of the Pentagon's sprawl. The security was oppressive, a multi-layered ritual of biometric scans, armed escorts, and the confiscation of his cell phone and laptop. It felt less like an office and more like entering the sanctum of American power.

General Milley's secretary, a woman with the poised stillness of a veteran agent, welcomed him with a nod and led him to a waiting room. Five minutes later, she opened the heavy oak door to the General's office.

Milley stood before a large, unadorned desk, waiting. "Aadil. Thank you for coming." He gestured to a leather chair. Once they were seated, he leaned forward, his hands clasped. "The work you've done over the last four years it's changed the game. Because of your intelligence, our teams are acting on leads we haven't had in eight years. For the first time since Tora Bora, we feel we can win this hunt. We are close to Bin Laden."

He let the weight of that statement fill the room. "You are a significant asset to the United States. I don't know if it will be next year or the year after, but the end is in sight. We've already apprehended several key facilitators, men close to him. That success belongs to you. And when this mission concludes, we have a new task for you. No rush, but it's a proposal that, frankly, is more classified than the Bin Laden operation. The rewards are commensurate. This stays between us. You may tell your wife, but no one else."

"I understand, sir," Aadil said, his voice even. "You have my confidence."

"Good." The General's gaze intensified. "What do you know about the Pakistani nuclear program?"

"I know Pakistan is a nuclear power. That's common knowledge."

"The heart of their program," Milley continued, "is buried in the mountains near Islamabad, in a place called Kahuta. Heard of it?"

"Yes, sir. By name only. I've never been."

"We have a strategic interest in neutralizing that program. The ISI and Pakistani Army have a stranglehold on security there. We need a local asset, someone who can help us gain access. You would have the full, combined support of the CIA, Mossad, and RAW. The Israelis and Indians are with us on this. We would protect you."

Milley leaned back, a calculated move. "We know you have the capability. We already have people inside the Pakistani military. And as for the political will, every Pakistani politician, including the Prime Minister, is in our pocket."

Aadil feigned mild curiosity. "And if the Prime Minister changes?"

"It makes no difference," Milley stated flatly. "We are the ones who approve who leads that country. Without American consent, no government in Islamabad survives. We control their finances, their politicians, their judges, their generals. We have a file on every one of them, their secrets, their weaknesses, their price."

"Let me think about it," Aadil said, keeping his reaction carefully neutral. "My priority, and Ashley's, is to finish the current mission. We can discuss the next task after that."

"Of course," Milley nodded, handing him a discreet card. "Take your time. This has my direct, secure email. Reach out if you need anything. Let's reconvene in March."

Ashley was waiting for him, her anxiety palpable. "Well?"

"The Pentagon is pleased," Aadil said, shedding his jacket. "They've arrested some key Taliban members based on the leads we provided."

"Your leads," she corrected him pointedly. "Were they the same ones who left you for dead?"

"The same. I'm glad they're in a cage." He took a deep breath. "And as I guessed, Milley wants me to lead an operation against the Pakistani nuclear program."

Ashley's face paled. "Aadil, that's... that's a suicide mission. What did you say?"

"I told him I'd think about it and discuss it with you."

"Good answer," she said, her voice dropping to a whisper. "And just between us? I don't trust our own government. The CIA, the Army, they're involved in so much unnecessary shit. Just look at the 'weapons of mass destruction' in Iraq."

"I know," Aadil agreed. "I told the General our first responsibility is to finish the Bin Laden mission. Then we're done."

"Agreed, one hundred percent," Ashley said, a wave of relief washing over her. "Thank God we have our savings. We have the house in Pakistan, and my mom's place, we're set. We don't need this."

"Maybe we could buy a place here?" Aadil suggested changing the subject to a safer dream. "A cabin in the mountains, perhaps?"

Ashley's eyes lit up. "I've always loved Colorado. Let's go next weekend. A long weekend. We can look around."

For the next week, they lost themselves in fantasy, searching for cabins near Denver and Colorado Springs. They envisioned a $500,000 retreat where they could escape for a few months each year. But when they discussed it with Ashley's mother, she offered a dose of financial pragmatism.

"Don't sink half a million into a cabin you'll use four times a year," she advised. "Think of the maintenance, the cleaning. Rent instead. You can experience different places without the anchor of a mortgage."

They saw the wisdom in her words. "She's right," Aadil said later. "We should be saving and investing. We can't count on Pentagon money forever."

Their trip to Colorado was a blessed distraction. The rugged peaks reminded Aadil of the northern areas of Pakistan, but with paved trails and a serene order that his homeland lacked. For four days, they hiked and dreamed, pushing the shadow of General Milley's proposal to the back of their minds. They returned to D.C. refreshed, but the looming decision waited for them, as solid and imposing as the fortress they had just left.

CHAPTER 28:
THE FINAL MISSION BEGINS

Aadil and Ashley returned home for a short four-day break. As always, Ashley dove straight back into her law firm, juggling her full caseload. Aadil, however, found himself preoccupied, his thoughts circling endlessly around the mission and the one name that had haunted him for years: Bin Laden.

This time, he sensed a change in the air. The ISI was far more alert than before. After the arrests of several of Bin Laden's close associates, Pakistani intelligence and the army had tightened their grip across the northern regions. Every movement was being watched, every unfamiliar face noted.

Still, Aadil's commitment to the U.S. government to find and confirm Bin Laden's location remained unshaken. He knew the risks, but he also knew he was too close to stop now.

One evening, a secure email arrived from General Milley. The message was brief:

"Aadil, I'd like your thoughts on the new regional tasking. Your experience and judgment are vital.

GM"

Aadil showed the email to Ashley. She smiled softly, then dictated a careful reply:

"General Milley,

I am focused on completing the current mission. I have not yet discussed future commitments with Ashley. Let me complete this assignment, and we will revisit the opportunity later.

Best regards,

Aadil."

It was decided that Ashley would not accompany him this year, either. Aadil alone would attend the Pentagon briefing in March.

At the meeting, they reviewed multiple strategies. The plan remained simple. Aadil would continue operating under his alias, Gul Khan, maintaining his business of selling wholesale food items across Afghanistan and northern Pakistan. His cover was perfect: a trusted trader with deep connections, invisible to outsiders.

His new objective was to extend his routes toward the city regions, keeping a close eye on the populated belt north of Islamabad.

Aadil knew it would be tougher this time. The ISI had learned to recognize patterns. Still, he was ready. He had survived far more dangerous assignments.

When his truck crossed into the border area through the Khyber Pass, the narrow, ancient gateway between Pakistan and Afghanistan, he immediately sensed the difference. The checkpoints were heavily fortified, and the guards were more aggressive. Each stop came with a barrage of questions.

Where do you work? Who buys your goods? Why are you traveling this route?

They inspected his ID, his passport, and his vehicle from top to bottom. His phone was checked too, though it contained nothing except the contact details of shopkeepers and suppliers.

Inside Pakistan, he realized he was being followed. The same type of white Suzuki van appeared more than once in his rearview mirror. ISI, no doubt.

Still, Aadil remained calm. He had trained himself not to flinch under scrutiny.

He was stopped again outside Abbottabad, a serene town nestled in the hills, roughly north of Islamabad, a place known for its quiet streets and its many retired army officers.

When questioned, Aadil explained smoothly.

"I'm a wholesale trader of rice, wheat, sugar, oil, spices, and lentils. I sell directly to the shopkeepers or local families."

The officers found nothing unusual in his truck or pickup. His demeanor was steady, his documents in perfect order.

They let him go.

Aadil drove away slowly, but his instincts were sharp.

Something about Abbottabad felt different.

CHAPTER 29: THE CALL THAT CHANGED EVERYTHING

One week later, Aadil's phone buzzed with an unknown number.

He hesitated before answering.

"Assalamu Alaikum, brother. Can you deliver sheep meat?"

The voice was calm, deep, and familiar. Aadil recognized it instantly. It was the same man who had called months earlier about Middle Eastern food supplies.

"Sheep meat?" Aadil repeated. "I've never done that before, but it can be arranged. I'll need a few large deep freezers to keep it frozen during transport."

"No problem," the caller replied quickly. "You'll be paid for the meat and the freezers. Our Ameer likes good quality sheep meat."

The word *Ameer* slipped out too easily. It struck Aadil like a spark.

He kept his voice steady.

"Insha'Allah, my brother. Tell me the date and place."

He expected a remote Afghan location, like all his previous deliveries.

But the answer stunned him.

"Not far. Just ten miles outside Abbottabad, after the toll bypass. Thursday morning."

Aadil's heart skipped. Abbottabad is a quiet military city surrounded by forested hills and guarded compounds.

He knew the route by heart:

Peshawar to Nowshera to the Hazara Expressway (E-35), then Haripur, Havelian, and Abbottabad.

Just before the city limits, the Salhad Toll Plaza marked the bypass. Beyond it, the road curved through pine trees and stone ridges, the kind of place where someone could live unnoticed for years.

Aadil had three days.

He purchased two commercial deep freezers, large enough to fit inside his Toyota Hilux pickup. He arranged for a local butcher to prepare five premium-quality sheep early Thursday morning.

That evening, he met Karim, Dr. Afridi's assistant, and explained the situation.

Karim's reaction was cautious but intrigued. "Buy the freezers. Keep your cover. We'll be watching."

Thursday came. The air near Abbottabad was cool, the highway wrapped in mist.

At the designated spot just past the toll bypass, a dark pickup truck was already waiting. The driver was a tall man with a trimmed beard and calm eyes. Several others stood nearby, watching silently.

They transferred the meat and both freezers from Aadil's truck to theirs. While helping lift one unit, Aadil discreetly slipped a small tracker beneath the rear axle of their pickup.

When the deal was done, the man handed him a thick envelope of cash, nearly five times the value of the meat and equipment.

"Our Ameer appreciates your service, brother. We'll need another delivery soon. Someone will call you on Saturday. You'll meet him in Peshawar."

"Anything illegal?" Aadil asked lightly.

The man smiled.

"No, no. Just supplies from Saudi Arabia. We trust you. We've watched you since last year, when you placed those posters. You are one of us."

"Alhamdulillah," Aadil replied, his voice steady. "If it's for our Ameer, I'll deliver it personally."

On Saturday morning, the call came as promised.

"Brother, can we meet near Peshawar Airport? About five miles out. We have the supplies ready."

"How large a load?" Aadil asked.

"A Hilux pickup will do. The items are from Saudi Arabia, food, spices, dates, and some other goods."

When he arrived, two men helped him load crates of Middle Eastern products, things rarely found in Pakistan: premium dates, canned stews, preserved meats, even Arabic coffee. It took nearly two hours.

The man supervising the loading smiled, wiping sweat from his forehead.

"You're strong, brother. Not many can load like that."

Aadil replied, "I've done this work all my life."

He made the four-and-a-half-hour drive to Abbottabad and delivered the goods there. The buyers handed him another bag full of cash, packed loosely in what looked like a pillow cover.

Aadil thanked them, returned to Peshawar, and immediately met Karim to report everything.

Karim listened intently, then smiled for the first time in months.

"Dr. Afridi will meet you tonight. He's certain of it now."

That evening, Dr. Afridi arrived at Aadil's residence. His expression was sharp and focused.

"Aadil, this confirms what we've suspected. Whoever ordered this shipment is not just anyone. These supplies came from Saudi Arabia, meant for someone of high status and secrecy. We're already tracking that pickup. The signal is active."

He paused, then added quietly, "If we're right, we may finally be closing in on Bin Laden."

CHAPTER 30:
THE LAST MEETING

It had been almost two and a half years since Aadil last met Dr. Afridi face-to-face.

The meeting took place quietly in a small guesthouse on the outskirts of Peshawar.

Dr. Afridi handed Aadil a sealed envelope, his yearly compensation in cash. Then he spoke, his tone low but urgent.

"Now listen to me carefully, Aadil. Things are going to get ugly, maybe in the next few days, maybe in the next few weeks. You've done enough. You're a Pakistani, and you've helped the U.S. government. That alone is enough to make you a target."

He paused, his eyes heavy with fatigue.

"My advice, as a friend, is to leave the country while you can. You have a good wife, someone who has already sacrificed so much for you. I don't want to see you end up in another prison, or worse."

Aadil stayed silent, absorbing every word.

"We are very close now," Afridi continued. "Closer than ever to Bin Laden. And it's because of you. The entire credit goes to your courage and your instincts. I may be the CIA's country director for this mission, but you, my friend, were the one who made it happen."

He exhaled slowly, the weight of years visible in his posture.

"I know your past," he said quietly. "I know you once worked for the ISI, and later as part of Sheikh Mohammed's own security, under ISI orders. I also know they turned on you, that you were never part of the 9/11 plot. You were following orders, doing your job."

"People like us," he added bitterly, "we work our entire lives in the shadows. No one knows what we've done. No medals, no recognition. We die as ghosts."

He looked directly into Aadil's eyes.

"I trusted you from the first day we met. And I was right. I don't know what will happen to me after this mission, but you still have a choice. You have a wife, a home, and a U.S. passport that can save your life."

A faint smile crossed his face.

"You're lucky. The Pentagon still needs you. Otherwise, they'd have erased your name by now, as they did to many others."

He stood and offered his hand, but Aadil embraced him instead.

"Allah hafiz, my friend," Afridi said softly. "Take care of yourself, and of Ashley. She's a rare woman. I've never seen anyone like her, a white American girl who gave up everything for love."

"Allah hafiz," Aadil replied, his voice thick with emotion.

The next morning, Aadil called Yasser and asked him to meet in Peshawar. Karim, Afridi's assistant, had already booked an evening flight to Dubai for him.

At the meeting, Aadil handed Yasser a bundle of cash and a sealed package.

"Deposit the money into my and Ashley's account, one installment each month, same as last year. And this package, send it to the ISI Chief, my old training officer, but only after Bin Laden's arrest. Keep it safe. Don't store it in our new house."

Yasser nodded solemnly. "I didn't know your training officer is now the ISI chief."

"Don't worry, brother. I'll handle it."

They hugged briefly before Yasser drove him to the airport.

"Be careful," Yasser whispered.

"Insha'Allah," Aadil said. "I'll call you and mother from the States."

Aadil landed in Dubai late that night. He took a taxi straight to his safe office, a small, unmarked room used by CIA assets, where he retrieved his American passport, IDs, and cash. He left behind his Pakistani documents, locking them away for good.

Inside the restroom, he shaved his beard, trimmed his hair, and changed into a crisp shirt and blazer. The rugged truck driver Gul Khan vanished from the mirror. Aadil Gul, the American citizen, looked back at him.

He pulled out his U.S. phone and called Ashley.

"I'm in Dubai," he said quietly. "Can you book me the next flight to D.C.? Either from Dubai or Abu Dhabi, whichever is faster. If not, I'll fly through Doha."

Ashley was already at her computer.

"Hold on," she said. "Give me five minutes."

Within moments, she found a first-class seat and confirmed the booking.

"You've got eighteen hours before departure," she said. "I'm booking your hotel near the airport now. Go there and get some rest."

"Thank you," Aadil said softly.

"It's done. I'll text you all the details. Just come home safe."

He smiled for the first time in weeks.

"Insha'Allah. I'm on my way."

As the call ended, Aadil leaned back into his chair, exhausted but relieved. He thought of Dr. Afridi's warning and his quiet confession of trust.

For the first time, Aadil realized how deeply that man had risked his own life to protect him.

Now, with the mission almost complete and Bin Laden's shadow looming over Abbottabad, Aadil knew one thing.

The next call from Langley would change everything, forever.

CHAPTER 31:
THE HIDDEN COMPOUND

Two days after Aadil arrived in Washington, D.C., a black SUV pulled up in front of his townhouse. Ashley was still at work, and Aadil had just finished his morning coffee when he noticed the tinted windows and discreet government plates.

General Milley stepped out. He was smiling, but his face was tense.

"Good morning, Aadil. I hope you're rested," he said.

"Yes, sir," Aadil replied calmly.

"Grab your jacket. We're going to Langley."

Aadil locked the door and followed him into the SUV.

The conference room at Langley was packed. Senior CIA officers, Pentagon liaisons, and several NSA intelligence analysts were seated around the table. Large screens displayed satellite images, coordinates, and heat maps of northern Pakistan.

When Aadil entered, the conversations stopped. General Milley motioned for him to sit.

A senior CIA analyst began the briefing.

"Three days ago, we picked up a tracker signal, frequency consistent with the one you placed under that pickup truck near Abbottabad."

"We've been tracing the signal ever since," another officer added. "It led us to a walled compound about a mile northeast of Bilal Town, Abbottabad. Roughly eight times larger than the surrounding houses."

A satellite image filled the screen. A high-walled structure with no phone lines, no internet cables, and barbed wire facing inward.

"This place doesn't exist on any local map," the analyst continued. "No land records, no registration. The residents burn their trash inside the courtyard, and the upper balconies are covered with canvases."

General Milley turned to Aadil.

"Does it look familiar?"

Aadil studied the image. The mountain ridge, the small dirt road, and the distance from the Toll Bypass.

"Yes," he said slowly. "That's the same route where I made the sheep meat delivery. The same man picked it up."

"You're sure?" Milley pressed.

"One hundred percent," Aadil replied. "That's where the pickup went."

Dr. Afridi's name came up next. The team had been coordinating with him through encrypted channels. He had recently collected DNA samples from children inside the compound under the cover of a vaccination campaign.

A female analyst looked up from her laptop.

"We compared the DNA with Bin Laden's known family members."

She paused.

"It's a match."

The room went silent.

General Milley stood up, his tone shifting from cautious to decisive.

"Gentlemen, we've got him."

Everyone in the room understood what that meant. Ten years of searching, hundreds of missions, and billions spent on intelligence.

Now, thanks to Aadil's tracker and Afridi's confirmation, Osama Bin Laden had finally been located.

Milley turned back to Aadil.

"You just closed the biggest manhunt in modern history."

Aadil remained quiet, his expression unreadable. He wasn't celebrating. He was remembering the dusty road, the men who trusted him, and the quiet voice that said, "Insha'Allah, brother."

The next phase of the meeting was led by a tall man in a Navy uniform, Admiral McRaven.

"We're launching a covert strike under JSOC, codename Operation Neptune Spear. Two stealth Black Hawks, SEAL Team Six, no Pakistani notification. You all know the risk."

A large digital clock appeared on the screen, counting down from D minus five.

"Aadil," McRaven said, "you'll stay here as an observer. You've already done your part. Once it's confirmed, your extraction identity will be finalized. New location, new name, permanent cover."

Aadil nodded. He had already accepted that part of his life was over. Gul Khan, Afghanistan, the checkpoints, all of it.

That evening, Aadil and Ashley sat together on the balcony of their D.C. apartment. The city lights shimmered below, and the autumn wind carried the faint hum of traffic.

Ashley rested her head on his shoulder.

"So… this is it?" she asked softly.

"Almost," he replied. "If everything goes right, it ends tomorrow night."

"And if it doesn't?"

"Then there will be a war," he said quietly. "But I believe it will end."

She looked at him, her eyes full of both fear and pride.

"I'm proud of you, Aadil."

"No," he said gently. "You should be proud of us. You saved me when no one else did."

They sat in silence for a while, two people bound by secrets, sacrifice, and love.

CHAPTER 32:
D-DAY – LANGLEY COMMAND CENTER

May 1, 2011.

The operations room at Langley was dimly lit, filled with monitors and military personnel. Aadil sat near the back, his eyes fixed on the live feed from Abbottabad. General Milley, Admiral McRaven, and the President were connected through secure communications. The SEAL team was approaching the compound.

In the White House Situation Room late that evening, the atmosphere was electric, a mix of exhaustion, anxiety, and history in the making. Around the long, polished table sat the President, the Vice President, the Secretary of Defense, the CIA Director, the Chairman of the Joint Chiefs, and key members of the National Security Council. On the central screen, satellite images of Abbottabad glowed: the compound, the walls, the mysterious third-floor balcony.

The President leaned forward.

"We're ready. But one question remains," he said quietly. "Do we inform the Pakistani Army before the raid?"

The room fell silent.

The Secretary of State spoke first. "Pakistan is a partner on paper. If we strike without notice, it violates their sovereignty. It could destroy our alliance."

The CIA Director responded immediately. "Sir, with respect, the ISI has leaked before, repeatedly. If they know even ten minutes early, Bin Laden will vanish again."

The tension thickened. Half the room nodded one way, half the other.

"Let's take a count," the President said. "Those in favor of notifying Pakistan?"

Hands rose slowly: the Secretary of State, the Defense Secretary, and a few others.

"Against?"

The CIA Director, General Milley, and the National Security Advisor raised theirs.

The vote was evenly split.

General Milley broke the silence.

"Mr. President, Pakistan's military is competent. If they think our helicopters are an attack, they'll respond. We're talking about F-16s in the air within minutes. We can't afford that."

He paused, then added, "But if we tell them too soon, ISI might warn the compound. We lose everything."

The President exhaled, deep in thought.

"So, what's your recommendation, General?"

"Notify them, but not until we're already in the air, thirty minutes before impact. That's enough time for them to stand down air defenses, but not enough to leak."

The CIA Director nodded reluctantly. "That's a risk I can live with."

The President scanned the room, reading every face.

"And the Pakistani Army Chief? Will he cooperate?"

Milley nodded. "Yes, sir. General A.K. has maintained back-channel contact with us through the defense attaché. I'll handle it personally."

The President gave a slight nod. "Do it. Quietly."

Within the hour, from the Pentagon's secure line, General Milley placed a coded call to Rawalpindi. General A.K., the Chief of Army Staff of Pakistan, answered from his private office.

"General A.K., this is Milley. We're about to conduct a precision operation near Abbottabad. Target: a high-value terrorist. No Pakistani targets. No threat to your forces. We request only that your air defenses stand down for the next two hours."

There was a long pause.

Then General A.K. replied calmly. "General Milley, officially, I do not hear this call. But unofficially, understood."

He lowered his voice. "Our radars will not engage. You will have clear airspace. But we cannot take public responsibility."

"Understood," Milley replied.

General A.K. added carefully, "The Pakistani people will be furious if they believe we cooperated. We will tell the media that your forces acted without our knowledge, just as we do for the drone strikes."

Milley allowed a faint smile. "We both know how this works. Thank you, General."

"Good luck, General Milley. May it be quick and clean."

The line went dead.

Back in the Situation Room, Milley turned toward the President.

"We're cleared, sir. Pakistani air defenses will stand down. Publicly, they'll deny everything."

The President nodded. "That's the deal we expected. We take the risk, we take the heat, but we bring justice."

He slowly stood, his eyes fixed on the satellite screen showing the compound once more.

"All right. Launch the mission."

A single red light blinked on the screen.

Operation Neptune Spear was active.

At 00:30 Pakistan time, one of the Black Hawks crash-landed inside the compound walls, but the mission continued. Gunfire erupted, movement flashing on the infrared cameras. The room at Langley was tense, silent, breathless.

Then the radio crackled.

"For God and country. Geronimo EKIA."

Enemy killed in action.

Everyone exhaled.

Aadil lowered his head, whispering a quiet Alhamdulillah.

General Milley placed a hand on his shoulder. "You did it, son. You closed the chapter."

Hours later, Aadil stood outside Langley, watching the first light of dawn break across the sky. He knew the world would soon learn the news, but his name would never be mentioned.

He pulled out his phone and sent Yasser a single line of text.

"Mail the package."

Then, looking up at the morning sky, he murmured, "It's over, Doctor. You were right. We live unknown, and we die unknown."

He turned and walked toward the waiting car, toward a new identity and a life that would never truly belong to anyone but the shadows.

Six weeks had passed since Aadil returned to Washington. To the public, the story was simple: Osama Bin Laden was killed in Abbottabad. But behind the headlines, the situation in Pakistan had exploded.

CHAPTER 33:
ISI RETALIATION

In Islamabad, the Director General of Inter-Services Intelligence, General A.P., sat in his dark office, slamming his fist against the table. Files were scattered everywhere: photos, satellite maps, and intercepted communications.

"How the hell did they do this under our noses?" he shouted. "Abbottabad. In the middle of our military zone."

His officers stood silent, their faces pale. The humiliation was global. Pakistan's military had been bypassed, its sovereignty violated, and its top intelligence service ridiculed.

General A.P. paced the room. "Find every contact, every driver, every doctor, every contractor who worked with foreigners in the last five years. I want answers."

Within twenty-four hours, the ISI launched Operation Clean Sweep, a massive internal crackdown across Peshawar, Islamabad, and the tribal regions.

The first targets were the UNO field offices and foreign-funded NGOs operating near the Afghan border. ISI teams stormed warehouses, seized files, and detained dozens of aid workers. By the end of the week, every UNO supply office in Peshawar, Chitral, and Khyber Agency had been shut down. The pretext was national security. The real reason was the search for Gul Khan.

In a hidden ISI briefing, one officer spoke cautiously. "Sir, the description fits the driver who made multiple supply runs between Dubai, Peshawar, and the Afghan border. He used both Pakistani and Emirati IDs. Locals knew him as Gul Khan."

General A.P.'s eyes narrowed. "Find him. I want his entire network. Anyone he ever talked to."

It took the ISI nearly two months to piece everything together. From surveillance photos, checkpoint records, and phone intercepts, they traced a pattern: a truck driver with unusual cross-border permissions, frequent trips to Dubai, and close links to a medical NGO headed by Dr. Afridi.

"It's the same man," an ISI officer reported. "He was a CIA undercover operative, an American citizen. Real name: Aadil Gul."

General A.P. closed his eyes for a moment, then spoke quietly. "He played all of us, and he succeeded."

Two days later, ISI commandos raided Aadil's house in Peshawar. It was empty. Every drawer, every wall, every hidden compartment revealed nothing. Neighbors said he had left weeks earlier. A few old receipts, one faded Quran, and an empty safe were all that remained. In frustration, one officer smashed the safe open, but there was only dust.

General A.P. stared at the report and muttered, "He cleaned everything. Professional."

Meanwhile, Karim, Dr. Afridi's loyal assistant, had been moving from safehouse to safehouse since Aadil's departure. He knew they were coming. On a rainy night near the outskirts of Peshawar, his vehicle was ambushed by an ISI tactical team. A brief gunfight erupted, and Karim was hit twice in the chest.

Before he died, he whispered to the officer standing over him, "You're too late. It's already done."

His phone was destroyed, and his papers burned. The ISI found nothing useful, but they understood what his last words meant. Bin Laden was gone, and nothing could undo it.

Dr. Afridi was arrested within a week. He was charged with treason, espionage, and collaborating with foreign intelligence agencies. His face appeared on every Pakistani news channel, branded as the man who betrayed the nation. He was locked in an underground cell, cut off from the world.

Only General A.P. visited him once. "You worked for the Americans," the General said coldly.

"No," Afridi replied weakly. "I worked for the truth."

"Truth doesn't exist in this business, Doctor," the General said. "Only sides."

He turned and walked away. That was the last time anyone saw Dr. Afridi in public.

In Washington, Aadil watched the news in silence. Ashley sat beside him, horrified by the reports of arrests and killings in Pakistan.

"They're blaming everyone," she said quietly. "Even the UNO."

"I know," Aadil replied. His voice was calm, but his eyes were heavy.

"Karim?" she asked.

Aadil nodded slowly. "He's gone."

They sat without speaking for a long time.

"Do you ever regret it?" Ashley asked, finally.

"No," Aadil said after a pause. "But I'll never forget it."

He stood, walked to the window, and looked out at the city skyline, free, bright, and distant.

"In this line of work," he whispered, "you don't win. You survive a little longer than the others."

CHAPTER 34:
THE DISAPPEARING SHADOWS

Islamabad — Two Days Before the Raid

Dr. Shahid Afridi had seen enough in his life to recognize the scent of danger long before it arrived. Years of working with intelligence networks, the CIA, aid agencies, and local operatives had sharpened his instincts beyond reason. Something was coming. Something big.

The faintest changes told him everything: a few unusual cars parked near the UNO compound, new faces in the street and tea stalls, and encrypted signals appearing on radio frequencies that were usually silent. He did not need a message from Langley to know. The ISI was closing in.

For years, his organization, the G Foundation, had operated as a front, officially for polio eradication. In truth, it was a humanitarian mask covering the CIA's most sensitive mission: the hunt for Osama bin Laden. Dr. Afridi's compound near the diplomatic enclave looked ordinary, busy doctors, white vans, medical supplies, but beneath it, behind a reinforced door in the basement, sat a fully equipped communications hub. That basement connected Pakistan's soil to the Pentagon's war rooms.

Now, he knew it had to vanish.

He called only his most trusted assistant, Karim.

"It's time," Afridi said quietly.

"Time for what, sir?"

"To disappear."

Together, they worked all night. Every hard drive was pulled. Every encrypted chip was melted in a small furnace used for sterilizing needles. The communication arrays, servers, antennas, and data cables were smashed and packed into steel containers. He supervised every step, calm but relentless.

By dawn, the UNO headquarters stood hollow, a ghost building. Not a trace of their real purpose remained.

Afridi walked through the empty hallways, the echoes of his footsteps following him like memories. He touched one of the walls and whispered, "We did what we came to do. Now it's time to vanish."

By the following evening, every remaining file, photograph, and medical record had been burned. The office keys were returned to the landlord under the pretext of a budget suspension. The guards were dismissed. The white vans were sold. The G Foundation ceased to exist.

That night, Afridi stood on the rooftop, watching the lights of Islamabad fade into darkness. He thought about Aadil, his most trusted field man, now safely out of the country.

"At least one of us made it," he murmured.

He knew the ISI's response would be swift and unforgiving once the Americans struck. Within days, maybe hours, arrests, raids, and disappearances would sweep across Peshawar, Abbottabad, and the tribal belt. He had done all he could: protect his people, destroy the evidence, and buy time.

By dawn, Dr. Afridi was gone.

No trace. No phone signal. No trail.

Some said he crossed into the tribal region disguised as a local doctor. Others claimed he escaped toward the Afghan border under CIA protection. But no one really knew.

All that remained was an empty building and a few vaccine boxes marked with the faded logo of the G Foundation.

CHAPTER 35: FALLOUT

Islamabad, Pakistan — Morning After the Raid

The city was still half asleep when the red phones started ringing. Within an hour, Pakistan's Prime Minister had called an emergency National Security meeting. Across Rawalpindi, the Chief of Army Staff ordered every Corps Commander to report immediately. The news had broken worldwide: Osama Bin Laden was killed in Abbottabad by U.S. Navy SEALs. For Pakistan's military and intelligence establishment, it was nothing short of humiliation.

Around the oval table sat the country's most powerful men: the Chief of Army Staff, the Director General of ISI, more than twenty Corps Commanders, and their Personal Staff Officers. The Chief of Army Staff began, his voice steady but heavy.

"Gentlemen, this is an unprecedented day in our history, and not in a good way."

He paused.

"The Chief of Staff of the United States Army called me last night. He informed me of a covert mission after their helicopters were already in the air. I chose to cooperate quietly to avoid confrontation, and I stand by that decision."

He looked around the room.

"Let's be honest. Bin Laden had been a burden to us. We protected him for years under complex circumstances. But he became a constant source of pressure and liability, and a constant source of global blame. We did what we had to do."

A murmur rippled through the hall, shock, dismay, agreement, and resentment mixing together.

Then the Director General of ISI rose to speak.

"I take full responsibility for our security failure. The Americans penetrated deep into our airspace without detection. But I agree with the Chief. Bin Laden was of no value to us anymore."

He exhaled and folded his arms.

"And I no longer trust the Taliban. They have their own agenda, and some factions are now in direct contact with RAW."

He gestured toward his aide, who placed a sealed folder on the table.

"Last night I received a package from an old student. It contains proof that certain Taliban groups are being trained and funded by RAW agents across the Afghan border. These same networks are behind the suicide bombings that have killed more than a hundred thousand of our people, soldiers, civilians, and even leaders like Prime Minister Bhutto."

The generals leaned forward as documents and photographs were projected onto the wall: training camps, coded communications, and smuggling routes.

The Director General of ISI continued, informing them that, according to his former student, the so-called Triangle had been attempting to destabilize Pakistan's provinces. Everyone in the room understood the Triangle and its activities in Baluchistan.

"We must take strong measures to protect Baluchistan and the NWFP. It is essential to act decisively against all foreign agencies working against our country's interests. Unfortunately, some Baloch tribes have been cooperating with these agencies for personal gain."

He paused before adding, "The man who sent this information is the same individual who helped the CIA and Pentagon locate Bin Laden. He did not betray Pakistan. On the contrary, he gave us intelligence we now possess."

The room fell silent. A few heads nodded in grim respect.

"We will use this data to track every insurgent, every handler, every call. From now on, no one, not RAW and not the Taliban, will bleed this country again without paying the price."

Later that evening, the Director General of ISPR, the military's public voice, faced a wall of flashing cameras.

"The United States conducted this operation independently," he told reporters. "Pakistan was not informed in advance. The American helicopters used advanced stealth materials and low-altitude flight paths to evade radar. That is why they went undetected."

Officially, Pakistan denied all cooperation. Unofficially, everyone in the upper ranks knew the truth.

Across the ocean in Washington, D.C., the world was celebrating. Crowds filled the streets outside the White House, chanting, "USA! USA!" For America, justice had been delivered.

Inside a quiet Pentagon office, Aadil and Ashley sat across from senior officials. A single check lay on the table, fifty million dollars, marked Confidential Payment, Counterterrorism Operations.

"Your names will remain classified," the official said. "You're heroes, just not the kind who appear on television."

Ashley smiled faintly. Aadil nodded, grateful but exhausted.

"Without you," the man continued, "this mission wouldn't have happened. The Pentagon and the CIA thank you deeply."

As they left the building, Ashley squeezed Aadil's hand.

"It's finally over," she whispered.

"Yes," he said, gazing at the evening sky. "At least for now."

One month later, in their quiet suburban home, the email notification pinged softly on Aadil's laptop.

From: Gen. Milley@pentagon.mil

Subject: Future Mission Discussion

Let's meet next week. There's more work ahead.

Aadil closed the screen slowly, his reflection faintly visible against the monitor's glow. He turned to Ashley, who was making tea.

"It seems," he said softly, "our story isn't over yet."

THE END